S0-BEG-763

Dear Reader,

It is so nice to be back in fictional Jasper, Montana, with the Landry Brothers! And I must tell you how very much I appreciate all the support and letters forwarded to me while you patiently waited for Chance and Val's story.

Writing *Bedside Manner* allowed me to put my own spin on one of my very favorite films—the 1944 classic *Gaslight*. Though we all have people that we *think* drive us crazy in our lives, Chance Landry has the real thing. As a lay person, I had to do some homework on all the medical stuff, but that's always one of the fun parts.

What fun would torturing a doctor be if I couldn't give him a strong counterpart in Valerie Greene? They don't see eye to eye on much of anything, and she isn't the least bit shy about voicing her opinions.

I need to take a minute to thank Melissa Jeglinski, my very fabulous editor, and Denise O'Sullivan, Harlequin Intrigue senior editor, for their faith and compassion. Through the worst situations imaginable, they offered encouragement and guidance for which I will be eternally grateful.

I love to hear your comments. I hope you enjoy this trip into the wilds of Montana. Feel free to write to me c/o Harlequin Books, 233 Broadway, 10th Floor, New York, New York 10279. Or if you're on the Web, stop by www.KelseyRoberts.com or www.eHarlequin.com.

Regards,

Kelsey Roberts

KELSEY ROBERTS

BEDSIDE MANNER

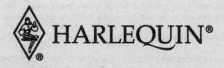

HARLEQUIN®

TORONTO • NEW YORK • LONDON
AMSTERDAM • PARIS • SYDNEY • HAMBURG
STOCKHOLM • ATHENS • TOKYO • MILAN • MADRID
PRAGUE • WARSAW • BUDAPEST • AUCKLAND

ISBN 0-373-88601-2

BEDSIDE MANNER

Copyright © 2004 by Rhonda Harding Pollero

ABOUT THE AUTHOR

Kelsey Roberts has penned more than twenty novels, won numerous awards and nominations and landed on bestseller lists, including *USA TODAY* and the Ingram Top 50 List. She has been featured in the *New York Times* and the *Washington Post,* and makes frequent appearances on both radio and television. She is considered an expert in why women read and write crime fiction, as well as an excellent authority on plotting and structuring the novel.

She resides in south Florida with her family.

Books by Kelsey Roberts

HARLEQUIN INTRIGUE

*The Landry Brothers

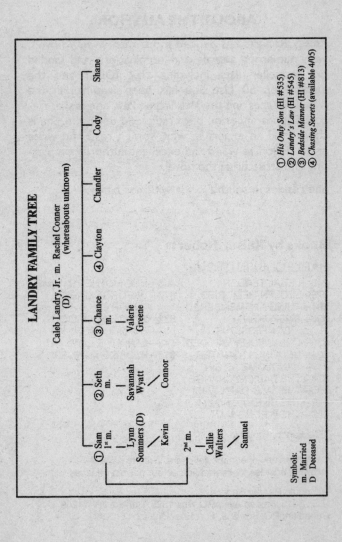

LANDRY FAMILY TREE

Caleb Landry, Jr. m. Rachel Conner (D) (whereabouts unknown)

① Sam
  1st m.
  Lynn Sommers (D)
  Kevin
  2nd m.
  Callie Walters
  Samuel

② Seth
  m.
  Savannah Wyatt
  Connor

③ Chance
  m.
  Valerie Greene

④ Clayton

Chandler

Cody

Shane

① *His Only Son* (HI #535)
② *Landry's Law* (HI #545)
③ *Bedside Manner* (HI #813)
④ *Chasing Secrets* (available 4/05)

Symbols:
m. Married
D Deceased

CAST OF CHARACTERS

Chance Landry, M.D.—The dedicated doctor has dated just about every single woman in Jasper, Montana, and broken his share of hearts. Could one of his ex-lovers be out to ruin his career by framing him for murder?

Valerie Greene—The Native American beauty works for Chance but refuses to fall for his charming bedside manner. Yet when Chance is framed, she comes to his defense. Is she harboring feelings stronger than those of a co-worker?

Harold Benton, M.D.—The chief of staff at Jasper Community Hospital has a long history with Chance. Could his jealousy over the other man's success have led to murder?

Miss Halloway, RN—Chance's nurse likes to gossip.... Does she also like to kill?

Tara Bishop—The quiet billing clerk always fades into the background, but what is she really hiding behind her mousy demeanor?

Seth Landry—The town sheriff, Seth is convinced of his brother's innocence. Still, duty may force him to arrest his own flesh and blood.

Clayton Landry—Currently serving life in prison for a crime he didn't commit. But none of the Landrys will rest until Clayton's name is cleared.

Shane Landry—The youngest Landry brother is hiding a few secrets of his own.

Dad, thanks for teaching me to
walk without your hands.
In loving memory:

Conway Trott Harding
February 2, 1929–January 5, 2003

Chapter One

Dr. Chance Landry was in his office dictating notes about the patients he had seen that morning. In spite of the tedium of his chore, he couldn't stop smiling.

One of his patients had been his sister-in-law Savannah. It had been his great pleasure to tell her she was carrying his brother Seth's child. Savannah had made him promise not to say a word. She knew that Jasper, Montana, was a small town and she didn't want some gas station attendant telling Seth first.

His very large family was getting very much larger. Earlier in the year, his oldest brother, Sam, and his wife, Callie, had welcomed a baby boy, Samuel Sheldon Landry. He was their second son. The baby was called

Sheldon. No one would dare refer to the baby as Junior, in Sam's and Callie's presence—or out.

His cousin Cade and his wife Barbara had a seven-month-old, Jackson Prather-Landry. Chance tensed when he thought about Jack's birth. Apparently, the boy was as impatient as his father, because he had come into the world almost three months early. Luckily, the neonatal unit in Helena was able to nurse him through those first few difficult months.

Speaking of nurses, Chance checked his watch. He had a date with a particularly fetching redheaded nurse this very evening.

He picked up another file and tried to decipher his own scripted notes. It was no wonder Valerie was always on his case. His handwriting had become atrocious in his thirty-five years on Earth. He set the file aside. He'd have Val translate it for him later.

His mind conjured a picture of his assistant, Valerie Greene. She'd been with him for six years, but he really didn't know much about her. Except that she had a killer body and an incredibly exotic face. He knew she was part Native American, which wasn't all that uncommon in Montana. He knew she had completed medical school and then bailed after her internship. But he didn't know why. He knew she believed in holistic medicine and some of the tribal cures she had learned as a child.

Val's homemade remedies were basically harmless, so he didn't care that she often handed them out along with his traditional advice to his patients. She was a puzzle to him. He wasn't being vain when he said she was the only woman who had never come on to him. Thanks to the wonderful Landry genes, Chance was a pretty good-looking man. That, coupled with the fact that he was a doctor, seemed to draw women to him without requiring much effort on his part.

And he did love women. All women. Well, all except for one. She was the reason he'd go to his grave single and without a family. Some part of him still felt the pain of her abandonment deeply. The other part was afraid that he would repeat her actions.

Val stuck her head in the door. Her eyes, which he noted were an incredible kaleidoscope of colors that included greens, golds and browns, appeared troubled. He hoped it wasn't an emergency walk-in.

"Is someone here?" he asked.

She shook her head as she entered the office. "Stop turning the ringer off on your phone," she chided as if he were some delinquent child.

Funny, she was the only one in the office who spoke to him with such candor. Maybe that was why he liked having her on his staff.

"The hospital is calling—pick up line one. You've got a major problem."

"What kind of problem?" Chance asked, annoyed. The small, local hospital just outside of town often classified something as simple as a hangnail as a dire emergency.

"The kind that can end your career as a doctor."

SEVEN and a half minutes later, Chance turned sideways to race through the glass doors of Jasper Community Hospital's emergency room. Val was at his side as he jogged to the nurse's station.

"Kent Dawson?" he asked.

"Exam area three."

Val reached the room ahead of him, shoving back the curtain, revealing a chaotic scene.

Chance muffled a curse as he pushed his way to his patient's bedside. In a matter of seconds, he had assessed the readouts on the machines, as well as the general condition of Mr. Dawson.

"When did you start the epinephrine drip?" he barked at no one in particular.

"Twenty minutes ago."

"Speed it up," Chance instructed. Dawson's pulse and respiration weren't good. He was covered in large red welts and his tongue was dangerously swollen. Chance met the man's frightened eyes and offered a reassuring glance.

Val took hold of Kent's hand and began to stroke it gently. As usual, her touch had a calming effect on his patient.

"Don't worry, Mr. Dawson," he heard Val soothe in her soft, mesmerizing tone. "You had an allergic reaction. Dr. Landry will have you comfortable in no time."

Chance hoped that was true. Dawson's anaphylactic shock was one of the worst cases he had ever seen.

The stench of Dr. Harold Benton's designer knockoff cologne battled the antiseptic smell of the examination area. Chance swallowed a groan. He wasn't in the mood for what he knew would be an unpleasant exchange between himself and Benton. The animosity they had shared in medical school had never abated. Chance had bested Benton in almost every rotation during their residency, and Benton held a grudge. It was ludicrous. Chance was happy in general practice. There wasn't any good reason for Benton to continue the childish air of competition.

Benton grabbed up the chart and began rifling through the pages. "What the hell were you thinking, Landry?" Benton challenged.

Chance ignored him long enough to be satisfied that the intervention was counteracting the symptoms. Dawson's respirations and pulse were returning to normal levels.

"It says right here on the chart that the patient is allergic to iodine," Benton continued.

Assured that his patient was stable, Chance ripped the chart away from Benton and scanned the contents. "This isn't right," he murmured. "I ordered a GI workup, *not* a contrast angiogram."

Benton crooked one finger and tapped the signature line. "You ordered an angiogram, *Dr.* Landry."

Chance was staring at his signature. He couldn't believe he had made such a potentially life-threatening mistake.

"Why don't you two take this outside," Val suggested.

Chance was more than willing. The last thing he needed was a lawsuit.

He leaned close to Val. There was something comforting about the way her long, dark hair smelled. Fresh and floral. He had no idea what herbs and berries she had smashed together to create the scent; he only knew that it had an oddly calming effect on his nerves.

"You could have killed that man!" Benton hurled the challenge like a gauntlet before they even reached the hallway.

"I didn't. And I didn't order the contrast angiogram."

Benton gave him a malevolent smile.

Chance wanted to give him a violent punch in response. But that wasn't an option.

"It must have been some sort of computer glitch," he guessed.

"Well, perhaps in the future you should review your orders *before* your laxness nearly kills someone."

"Perhaps," Chance steeled his eyes on Benton's narrow, ferretlike face, "you should go to hell."

AN HOUR LATER, Chance and Val were back at his office. Actually, it was an old Victorian house that Doc Gibbs had converted into a first-floor office with living quarters above. The place was much like Doc had left it years earlier, except for the computer system Val had insisted Chance install.

She followed Chance to the second floor. Val kept her eyes fixed on his broad shoulders and the way his well-worn denims hugged his impressive rear. As usual, she swallowed the desire to reach out and squeeze his buns. Chance didn't think of her in those terms. According to him, she was his co-worker, friend, buddy, trusted confidante.

In other words, she mused, *he thinks of me as a pal or a pet, not a specific gender.*

After climbing the narrow staircase, Val found herself in the inner sanctum. At least that's what it had been dubbed by her fellow workers. Val thought of it more as a love nest. Chance Landry was an active dater. No, she thought, a *very* active dater. He had pretty much worked his way through the eligible females in Jasper. He'd probably have to widen his search area now. And Val wondered, for the umpteenth time, why he had never once so much as asked her out for a cup of coffee. Six years and nothing more than a few working lunches and dinners.

It was annoying and something of a slap to her self-confidence. She was basically attractive. Had a sense of humor. Kept herself in good shape. Still, Chance looked right through her.

"Drink?" he asked as he gathered newspapers and journals off the round oak kitchen table, tossing them into a pile on the floor.

"Sure. What do you have?" She studied his profile while he studied the contents of his refrigerator. His thick, black hair was neatly trimmed. There were a dozen or so premature silver hairs gracing each temple. His face was simply a work of art. There was no denying that he had grown up in the harsh climate of Montana. Faint lines were etched into his deeply tanned face. She knew without looking that his best feature was those eyes. Eyes that could melt her to the core in less than thirty seconds. They were a beautiful mixture of blue and gray. She could only liken the color to that of a swift-moving, violent summer storm.

His eyes were a stark contrast to his welcoming, crooked smile. A smile only offered with his head slightly bowed. It was an odd quirk. But it somehow made the smile more appealing.

Chance held out a beer for her. She took it, then braced the top against the counter and smashed down hard to release the cap.

Chance laughed. "One of these days you're going to have to teach me to do that."

"Nope. A woman has to have some secrets."

"Except for you," Chance opined, turning those incredible eyes on her. "Though occasionally you annoy me, you are my closest friend. We don't have secrets between us."

Except for that minor little one about me

lusting for you. Val forced a smile and lifted her beer in a salute before taking a swallow.

Chance leaned against the counter. Pensively, he took a sip of his drink. "How in hell could I have screwed up so royally?"

Val stayed glued to her spot. It was a safe ten feet from Chance. "I'm sure it was some sort of computer thing."

"Computer or not, my signature was on the order."

"Then let's check the computer," she suggested.

Chance led her into the living room. It was an odd juxtaposition. Very masculine Chance surrounded by very delicate period furniture.

"This room is *soooo* you," Val teased.

"I lack redecorating initiative," Chance countered as he brushed off, then opened the notebook computer on the coffee table.

"You're supposed to use a computer, Chance, not dust it."

"I lack computing skills, too." He patted the spot next to him on the dainty, velvet-covered settee. "Come here and help me."

Helping him wasn't the top choice on her list, but she'd long ago learned to settle for friendship. Okay, maybe in her heart of hearts she didn't quite savor playing the role of his trusted pal. But there wasn't anything she could do about it.

Val's fingers flew over the keyboard. What she did in seconds would have taken Chance the better part of an hour. He respected her abilities. He also respected the fact that her thigh was touching his.

He felt like the worst kind of pig. She was working on his behalf and all he was focused on was the heat where her leg touched his. Chance shook his head, dismissing the thoughts in order to concentrate on the blue screen in front of him.

"This is too weird," Val said under her breath.

"It's a bunch of numbers," Chance commented.

He heard Val sigh deeply.

"It's codes," she explained. "I coded every procedure so that all that needs to be done is enter a patient name and the correct code and the printer spits out the appropriate order or prescription. I can even order office and medical supplies direct from the vendors."

"Do we have a screwup code?"

"No," Val continued to work feverishly on the machine. "This doesn't make sense," she murmured.

"My feelings exactly."

"No, look at this," she said, tapping the screen with her oval shaped fingernail.

Chance ignored the part of his brain that was focused on the pale peach polish. It was a stunning contrast to her olive-tinged skin. He read the information on the screen. "Dawson, Kent. Ulcer, pre-ops ordered, EKG, Chem. 7, GI Upper and Lower." He stroked the stubble on his chin. "That *is* what I ordered."

"Now look at this," Val said as she hit a couple of buttons on the keyboard. "Dawson, Kent, yada-yada, pre-op tests *and* a contrast angiogram."

"Why two orders?" Chance asked.

"Hang on," Val said, doing some more things on the computer. Her brow wrinkled and she turned her head, meeting his eyes. "According to this, you cancelled the original and substituted the second two nights ago."

"That's crap," Chance scoffed. "I could not have gone into the system to change orders.

Hell, I haven't even mastered playing solitaire yet."

Val rubbed her temple. "According to the network logs, the change was made at seven forty-five. from your desk terminal."

"Two nights ago at seven forty-five I was on my way to pick up a long-legged blonde."

"What's her name?" Val asked.

"Gretchen something," he replied. "Pretty as a picture and dumb as a stump."

"Your favorite qualities in a woman."

Chance heard the tinge of disapproval in her tone. "I wasn't asking her to marry me."

"No details, please. I'm sure I can guess what you were asking her to do."

"Lighten up, Val. I'm a healthy, single male. Not some crazed rapist. Besides, I never lead women on. I let them know from the start that I'm not a long-term guy."

"Commitmentphobic," Val corrected.

"Whatever. The point is, I couldn't have changed the orders. I wasn't even here."

"We'll verify it with your damsel du jour, then I can contact the tech people to fix this glitch."

"This glitch could have cost Kent his life."

"Just like anonymous sex could cost you yours."

Chance poked her in the ribs. "I do not have anonymous sex. I have brief, consensual, mutually gratifying physical relationships."

"Only because you choose to keep women at arm's length because you have never dealt with your issues concerning your mother."

"Yes, I have, and even if I haven't, I sure don't need your input on the subject."

"Fine. Spend your life afraid of commitment. Once your looks go, you'll be the lonely old guy sitting on the porch, pathetically cackling at disgusted young women on the street."

"I would not *cackle*," Chance insisted. "I plan on being a heartthrob forever."

"So did Marlon Brando," she quipped. "Back to work. We know there were two orders. How did your signature get on the bogus one?"

Chance shrugged. "I have no clue."

"You don't recall signing substitute orders?"

"I may not be computer-literate, but I do pay attention to what I sign."

"Which brings me back to—how did your signature get on the order?"

"I saw it," he said. "It was clearly on the chart in the hospital. My signature was at the bottom, in blue ink."

"This means you signed it."

"But I'm telling you that I didn't."

Val gave him a warning smile. "A heart-throb who also thinks he's perfect isn't a pretty combination."

"You think I did it? You think I screwed up?"

"I think it is possible that you made a simple mistake. It happens, Chance."

"Not to me."

"Well, the bottom line is that Mr. Dawson is fine."

"I know that," Chance admitted. "But that doesn't change the fact that I know I didn't order the contrast study. I've been treating Kent Dawson for years. I am fully aware of the fact that he has a potentially fatal allergy to iodine."

Val patted his leg. "And I am fully aware of the fact that you're human, Chance. Perhaps you had better cozy up to that idea."

CHANCE WAS slowly emerging from his foul mood by the following week. Val and Nancy

Halloway, his nurse, had made a point of not mentioning the Dawson mistake. Especially since Chance had verified that he was with the blonde of the day at the time the second order was written. How his signature got on the second order was still a mystery.

After a very busy morning, there was finally a lull in patients.

"Rock, paper, scissors?" Val suggested.

"I can go," Tara Bishop suggested.

Val and the nurse swiveled in their chairs to face the part-time billing clerk. Tara was very quiet. In fact, Val had dubbed her "the nontalker" about six months earlier. Well, that was true of her interactions with women. Whenever Tara was within ten feet of Chance, she became a babbling blob of stammered sentence fragments.

She seemed sweet, but she was so shy that Tara rarely—if ever—looked anyone in the eye. Needless to say, her unexpected offer to make a run for food was something of a surprise.

"Works for me," Val said, grabbing her purse from beneath the reception counter.

"Thanks, Tara," Nancy added. "Turkey on

rye toast, no mayo—I'm watching my waistline."

"Veggie pita for me," Val said. "And get Chance a rare roast beef with horseradish on a kaiser roll." Val pulled some crumpled bills out of her wallet. "That should cover it." She handed the money to Tara.

"Here is mine," Nancy added. "Throw in one of those gourmet chocolate chip cookies, too."

Val arched on brow. "No mayo but a thousand-calorie cookie?"

Nancy just shrugged. "So I'm watching my waistline *expand*."

"I'll be right back," Tara said. She slinked out of the office, barely making a sound.

"So, how was your weekend?" Nancy asked. At fifty-five and happily married, Nancy lived vicariously through her younger co-workers.

"Boring," Val admitted.

Nancy gave her a pitying look. "In a dating slump?"

"The well in Jasper has run dry. And I'm running out of ideas."

"What about a personal ad?"

Val laughed. "How many creeps do you

think would respond? I can see the ad now…
'Date wanted, non-smoker, noncriminal,
nonugly.'"

"You're just too picky," Nancy sighed. "I
have a wonderful nephew in Helena if you're
interested."

"I have a 'no blind date' policy. Sorry."

"For heaven's sake, Val, how are you ever
going to meet Mr. Right if you limit your
options?"

"I consider it limiting my revulsion. The
last time I was set up, the guy spent most of
dinner admiring himself in his reflection on
the back of the spoon. I spent two hours listening to him drone on about animal hus-
bandry. Then, and only then, did he insist we
split the check since his wife back in Utah
might get suspicious."

"Ouch."

"Yuck," Val corrected. "I'm ready to de-
cree that there isn't a normal single man in
Montana."

"It's a big state," Chance interjected. "Keep
looking."

She playfully offered him her tongue.
"Right, maybe I should start using the Chance

Landry rules of dating. What are those again?" she teased. "He has to have the IQ of a houseplant, has to have the looks of a *GQ* cover model but most of all, he must agree to a no-strings-attached liaison."

A strange look passed across Chance's face. It was gone before she could put a name to it.

"Those are guy rules. You need girl rules," he said.

"How double standard is that?"

Chance stroked his chin down to his throat. "I'm not being sexist, I'm being practical. You're a nurturer, Val. The scariest kind of woman, I might add. You need a guy who will appreciate you and your commitment to your community."

"Thanks, you make me sound like a mayoral candidate." Val sighed. "Come to think of it, I am the unofficial mayor of the Friend Zone."

"The Friend Zone?" Nancy asked.

"Sure. Every man I'm remotely close to thinks of me as one of the guys. They never look at me and think romantic thoughts. At this point, I am totally willing to consider a leer as a compliment and a potential step in the right direction."

"Men will never leer at you," Chance said.

Val's annoyance rose a notch or two. "Am I coyote ugly or something?"

"To the contrary," Chance answered. "You're exotically beautiful. Exotic beauty scares most men."

Exotically beautiful? She was glad she was seated. Hearing him say that about her made her weak-kneed and sent a shiver through her system.

"S-so that's your theory as to why my dating pool is shrinking?"

"You're beautiful and you're in the Danger Zone, not the Friend Zone."

Val looked at Nancy. "I can't wait to hear his explanation for this."

"It's true," Chance insisted. "You're entering the biological clock years. There's nothing worse for a guy than hearing that ticktock when you're lip-locked."

"Chance," Val groaned. "Not only am I *not* thinking about my biological clock, I've already hit the Snooze button on it. I'm not looking for Mr. Right. I'd be happy to settle for Mr. Right Now for the time being."

"And you say I'm the commitmentphobic in this group?"

Val hated having her words tossed back at her. "The difference between you and me is that I'm content with conversation and a nice meal. Apparently you, on the other hand, allow the conscienceless part of your anatomy guide you."

Chapter Two

"Did you leave your date in the car?" Shane asked without looking up from the action film he was watching.

"I don't have a date," Chance told his brother as he scooped up a handful of popcorn from Shane's bowl.

"Make your own!" Shane whined.

"This isn't burned, which means Taylor made it, not you."

"But she made it for *me*," Shane countered, moving the bowl out of reach. "I had to grovel for the better part of an hour to get it, so hands off."

"You were never good at sharing," Chance groused. "Once the baby brother, always the baby brother."

"You're the one acting like a baby," Shane

replied. "I'll assume your foul mood is because it's a Saturday night and studly ol' Chance doesn't have a date."

"You're an annoying pain in the ass, know that?"

Shane slid over to allow room for Chance to join him on the sofa in the living room of the ancestral home. The Lucky 7 ranch had been home to six generations of Landrys. Thanks to the marriages of two of his six brothers and one cousin, it appeared there would be a seventh generation to carry on the tradition.

"I live here," Shane countered. "You just have squatter's rights."

"Speaking of living here, where is everyone?"

"Sam and Callie are off with Seth and Savannah celebrating the coming issue of Seth's loins."

"You could sound happier."

Shane shrugged. "I would be if they'd taken Taylor along."

"I heard that!" came a sharp, female voice from the direction of the kitchen.

"You think I'm a pain? Try spending some time with Evil Housekeeper from Hell."

Chance chuckled. "I'm sensing tension here." He lowered his voice. "You got the hots for Taylor?"

Shane gave him a brotherly, one-handed shove. "I'd rather gnaw through my wrist and open a vein."

"Harsh, bro."

"You wouldn't say that if you lived here," Shane groused. "Taylor is one mouthy little wretch."

"An easy-on-the-eyes wretch," Chance shot back. "What's wrong, baby bro—did you finally meet your match?"

Shane scowled. "Not flaming likely. She lives to rag on me."

"You are such a whiner," Chance breathed. "Most guys would kill to have a housekeeper like her. I think she's attractive and sweet."

"That's why you get a beer," Taylor announced as she handed Chance a cold bottle. "You," she directed her words at Shane, "can get your own."

Chance thanked her and smiled. Taylor Reese was a pretty little wisp of a woman. She had wild blonde hair, cut in a blunt style. Every time he had seen her at the Lucky 7, her hair had been mussed. She always had that just-out-of-bed look. Any man would have been drawn to her, so what was Shane's deal?

"See?" Shane fairly cursed. "She's mean to me."

Taylor rolled her eyes. "Say please and I'll get you something."

"Please," Shane said in a huff.

Taylor left the room and returned in seconds with a hunk of smoked cheddar on a plate. "Here you go, Shane, some cheese to go with your whine."

"You're fired."

"You can't fire me. Only Sam can fire me."

Chance tried not to laugh. "I think she has you there, bro."

"Take her side," Shane sulked. "Everyone else does."

"No need," Taylor chirped happily, a devilish glint in her eyes. "I'm off to bed."

"Sleep well," Chance said.

"I hope she falls out of bed," Shane grumbled.

"You can be very childish," Chance pointed out. "Want me to get the name of a therapist? Sounds to me like you have…issues."

"Issue—*her*."

Silently, Chance wagered it would be a matter of months before his youngest brother married the waifish housekeeper.

"Speaking of women issues, how come you don't have a date on a Saturday night? Doesn't that break a streak or something?" Shane asked.

"I don't have a streak and I don't have a date by choice."

"Sick?"

"No! Why is my not having a date such a big deal?"

"Because you always have a date. Not having a date is like Lucy without Desi. It's like Burns without Allen. It's like Beavis without Butt-Head."

Chance gently slapped the back of his brother's head. "You're a jerk."

Shane rubbed his head. "I don't think that called for violence. Geez, Chance, what's got your shorts in a knot?"

Before he could answer, Shane stood, picked up the plate of cheese and went to the kitchen. He returned with a bottle of beer. Bracing it against the edge of the end table, he smacked the cap, sending it spinning on the wood floor.

"Where did you learn to do that?" Chance asked.

"Val." Shane took a long swallow.

"My Val?"

Shane cast him a suspicious look. "Didn't know you had staked a claim."

Chance felt a knot in his gut. "You two dating?"

Shane chuckled. "She's my friend. We get together a couple of times a month to watch videos."

"Just the two of you?"

"What are you? Her father?"

Chance told himself he was simply looking out for her welfare. "I just don't want to see her get hurt."

"Yeah, right," Shane chuckled.

"What's that supposed to mean?"

"The obvious," Shane replied. "I think you're hot for Val."

"I think you're mentally ill."

"Sorry, doc, but I've seen the way you look at her. And I've seen her. You two have everything in common."

"Hardly. She's too…nesting."

"Worse things could happen to a man than being married to a woman like Val."

Chance felt himself shiver at the *M* word. "That's my point. She needs someone who wants that stuff. Marriage, kids, yard, a 401K."

Shane was shaking his head. "You don't know her that well, then."

"How can you say that? We're together five and a half days a week. Sometimes more."

"Together *working*," Shane said pointedly. "Bet you didn't know she can kick my butt at poker. Or that she's a vegan. Or that she spends her Sundays out at the reservation giving free health care to her tribe."

Chance was perplexed by all the information Val had confided in his brother, but he wouldn't give Shane the satisfaction of knowing it. "I knew about the reservation. Where do you think she gets her supplies?"

"From you, but I'd bet my last dollar you never offered to help her."

"I didn't know she needed help. All she had to do was ask."

"She'd bite off her tongue before she asked

you. Val is a proud woman. She doesn't ask—she waits for volunteers."

"And you know all this because?"

"Because I've gone to the reservation with her a couple of times. I took some feed and some vet meds for their livestock."

Chance set back against the sofa. It was amazingly more comfortable than the old-woman furniture at his place. More comfortable for his body, but his mind was baffled. Val, as it turned out, was a far more complicated woman than he'd ever imagined. It piqued his interest and stirred places it should not have.

"WHAT ARE YOU doing here?"

Chance smiled at her. "I thought I'd ride out to the reservation with you."

Val raked her fingers through her dark hair with one hand, the other hand was clutching the edges of her robe. He would never have pegged her as the Victoria's Secret type, but there she was, just inches away, grand and glorious in peach silk. Shane was right; he didn't know Val at all.

"Come on in. I'll make some coffee."

Chance stepped inside the rustic cabin that she called home. Again, he was surprised. Instead of being all frilly and girly, it was casual and comfortable. Every piece of furniture was created by nature. The living room had chairs, a sofa and a coffee table, all made from bent hickory. In what he could see of the loft above, the theme continued. Her bed was a massive four-poster, made of roughly carved cedar. The only decorative items in the whole place were native folk art. Everything from totems to masks to sand paintings.

"This is great," he said when she emerged from the kitchen.

This time, she wasn't clutching her robe. His gaze instantly fell to the lace that encased her body. It was a hell of a body, too.

"I'll be dressed before the coffee is ready. Have a seat."

His eyes followed her up the wooden ladder to the loft above. Once she was out of sight, Chance fell into the sofa. He heard the shower start and soon the whole house filled with the scent of lavender. Knowing he shouldn't, Chance imagined peeling off that sexy nightgown and bathing her body in kisses. He continued to fantasize, placing himself in the shower with her, caressing and lathering her flawless skin.

He was suddenly warm. Very warm. And if he didn't change his train of thought, she'd know. When the water stopped, he threw a magazine in his lap and plastered a nonchalant expression on his face.

In what felt like seconds, Val bounded down the ladder in jeans and a sweatshirt. Though it was early summer, the morning temperatures were still barely above fifty.

Her wet hair was pulled back into a functional ponytail. It was a look Chance had never seen. Just as he had never noticed her high, sculpted cheekbones or the perfect arch of her brows. Having her hair back accentuated her unusual eyes. They were a hazel kaleidoscope rimmed in long, dark lashes. The trace of Native American blood gave them their interesting shape, large yet slightly almond.

Val went into the kitchen, praying her heartbeat would return to normal. Grabbing two mugs off hooks hanging over the sink, Val managed to fumble one, sending shards shattering everywhere. She muffled a curse.

"Stand still," Chance instructed. "I don't feel like suturing you if you step on this stuff. Don't you know it is much safer to wear shoes when in the kitchen?"

"Thanks for the tip," Val teased. She was trying to keep things light and professional. All that pretty much went to hell the instant Chance lifted her in his arms.

She could feel the hard muscle of his chest through her clothing. She hoped he couldn't feel the erratic beat of her heart. It was a battle to keep her breathing normal. Especially when she could smell his woodsy cologne. His hands seemed huge—at least the one bracing her back. It felt as if his fingers splayed from her waist to her shoulder blades. Mostly, it felt right.

"Where's the broom? I'll take care of the kitchen floor."

It took her frazzled brain a few seconds to remember what a broom was, let alone its location. *Lord, he must think I'm a ditz!* "Closet to the left of the stove."

"I'm an idiot!" Val criticized in a hushed tone once she was upstairs putting on her socks and tennis shoes. "Can I be cool, calm and collected? No, I have to break something, so he'll know I'm nervous. I should have just written that on my forehead in lipstick."

"All done," Chance yelled from below.

"Be right there." Val took several deep breaths to calm her frazzled state of humiliation. Sheer will enabled her to climb down and accept the coffee he offered. "Thanks."

"Black, the way you like it."

Val's heart landed squarely in her feet. "Actually, you take it black, I take light." *So much for fantasies.*

"Sorry."

Chance followed her into the kitchen. His chair scratched the floor as he pulled it away from the small table and sat down.

"That isn't cream," he said.

"It's soy," she explained. "All the benefits of milk without the animal fat."

"Anything 'without' something usually translates to 'without taste.'"

"Don't knock it until you've tried it. Want some breakfast?"

"Is it soy?" he asked.

"Fresh fruit with plain yogurt and a bagel."

"I'll take some fruit, no yogurt, and do you have any cream cheese for the bagel?"

"Imitation."

"Then skip the bagel."

"Fine, just don't complain when you're starving at eleven."

He had never seen her in a domestic setting. She seemed as comfortable in the kitchen as she was in an exam room. Sunlight streamed into the eat-in kitchen, casting beautiful highlights in her hair. It would be nice if her sweatshirt didn't fall to her thighs; he would have enjoyed watching a certain hidden part of her anatomy as she worked. She was right, he was a pig.

"Want to tell my why you showed up at my door at seven o'clock?"

"To go to the reservation with you."

"I've been going out there for years and you never seemed interested before."

She placed a plate of fruit in front of him. "Val, I'm doing something nice, so why the inquisition?"

"I'm not, I'm just wondering how it would have looked if I'd had company here."

"Did you?" He hated the fact that it

sounded more like an accusation than a question.

"No, lucky for you, my date last night goes to the top of my worst-dates-ever pile." She joined him at the table.

"What went wrong?"

She shrugged. "Everything."

He grinned. "So tell."

"You sound like Nurse Nancy."

"Do you tell Nancy all your secrets?"

She shook her head. "You never tell anyone *all* your secrets. It's bad form."

"Isn't that a little hard for you?" Chance asked. "I mean, you have a habit of saying whatever comes to mind."

She shook her head, then met and held his eyes. "There's a huge difference between telling your secrets and offering your opinion."

"Interesting hairsplit." It *was* interesting. Hell, suddenly everything about Val was interesting to him. It was like he was seeing her for the very first time. It was weird. Chance was suddenly paying attention to the smallest detail. It was a strange and annoying feeling. Val was his best friend. *No, Val was a woman.*

"So, who built this place?"

"Me."

Chance was stunned into a stupor. "You?"

Val cocked her head to one side, her lips pursed for an instant. "I take it you believe that a woman can't use a power saw *and* wear power shoes."

"I didn't mean it that way," he said, recovering slightly. "I'm just—"

"Surprised?"

"Impressed," he admitted freely. "I would never dream of trying to build a house on my own."

"That's because you're a Landry. Since I have to live off the salary you pay me, it was do it myself or live in some dinky apartment in town. It's not rocket science and I did have some help."

"From who?"

"Some of the men from the tribe. Why is this such a big deal to you?"

"I've never met a female construction worker."

"I'm not surprised, given the type of women you date."

Chance sat back in his chair. "What's that supposed to mean?"

Val's smile took his breath.

"Trophies, Chance. Remember Miss Rodeo Montana? If you can't, she's the one who longed for world peace and—my personal favorite—wanted to go to college to study modeling."

"She was nice."

"I'm sure she was," Val agreed. "But how do you have a conversation with someone whose only goal in life is to master the catwalk?"

"So she was a little shallow," Chance grudgingly admitted. "What about Peggy Mitchell from Helena. She was pretty *and* intelligent."

"And pretty easy," Val muttered. "Word around town is men have had more turns with her than a doorknob."

Chance winced, knowing full well that Val was right. "You're hardly in a position to judge me. You dated that salesman who happened to be married."

"Only one time and I didn't know he was married."

"What about Cliff at the Feed and Seed?"

Val gave him an elfin smile. "That was a mercy date. That doesn't count."

"Mercy date?"

"The guy you say you'll go out with just to get him to stop calling and begging."

"He still calls you."

"So he's thickheaded," Val explained. "Eventually he'll grasp the fact that I couldn't be less interested."

"Aren't you forgetting Hal Sommers?"

Val cringed. "Okay, that one was just a lapse in judgment."

"I could have told you the guy was a letch."

Her eyes narrowed. "Then why didn't you?"

Chance shrugged. "I guess I figured you knew what you were getting into."

"Thanks. If I would have known the guy assumed paying for dinner entitled him to a romp in my bed, I never would have gone. And Hal wouldn't be in line for the Vienna Boys Choir."

Chance laughed. "You put a hurting on him. It was all I could do the next morning when he came into the office swearing his bull had kicked him in the ba—groin."

Val laughed, too. "It was the only way I could get his…attention."

"Remind me not to piss you off."

"You can't help it," Val answered. "Your sexist proclivities guarantee you'll annoy me."

"I'm not sexist!" Chance insisted. "And the fact that I enjoy the company of beautiful women doesn't make me evil."

"You're right. It makes you lame. Come on, we've got a long drive ahead of us. Perhaps you could use that time to explain why you got this sudden burst of humanistic altruism."

Chance followed her out of the cabin. "I'm a doctor, by definition I'm a humanitarian."

"You're also a man, which most definitions makes you shallow. It's called Homecoming Queen Syndrome."

"Let's take my SUV. Shane put some feed in the back."

"Shane is so sweet."

"Shane's a prince," Chance agreed. "Does he have this Homecoming thing?"

"Nope. He doesn't put value on appearance alone."

"Like hell," Chance snorted as he transferred boxes from her Jeep to his truck.

"His housekeeper is beautiful and he doesn't think of her as a potential conquest."

"Shows what you know about my little

brother," Chance said, tapping the tip of his finger to her little nose. "Shane has the hots for Taylor in a big way."

Val blinked up at him.

"See, you don't know *everything*."

"Oh, blast!" Val cried out.

"What?"

"I forgot to take glucose sticks and insulin from the office. Beth Whitefeather needs those supplies."

"No problem. We'll detour to the office first."

"I can't believe I did that," Val said as she stepped up into the passenger seat."

"Maybe you were distracted by your big date."

"Maybe we could stop discussing our personal lives."

Chance didn't discuss it, but he was certainly thinking about it as he steered out of her driveway and onto the two-lane road that led to town.

The route was scenic and he never lost his appreciation for the snow-capped mountains framing the distance. He couldn't imagine life in a big city. Rural Montana was in his blood. Just like Val.

He wondered where that thought came from. He decided it was probably better not to delve too deeply into the reason for his newfound interest in his friend. Instead, he turned down the stereo and asked, "You ever think about leaving here?"

"Not an option," Val answered without hesitation. "I'm happy here, winter blizzards excluded. I loathe shoveling and I've never mastered the snowblower."

Chance was beginning to see how difficult it must be for her. She had to be strong and resourceful just to handle the winters. "I'm the king of snowblowing."

"Manual labor? You?" Val quipped.

"You seem to forget that I grew up on a ranch, Val. I've done more than my share of manual labor."

"Is that why you became a doctor?"

"Maybe, on some level. Mostly I wanted to accomplish something that was separate from my family."

"That's easy to do when you're loaded."

"You want me to apologize for having money?"

"Nope, I was just making an observation."

"How did you pay for med school?"

"The correct question is how much *am* I paying? I think I've got my loans down to about eighty-nine thousand."

He whistled. "That's a lot of debt."

"Tell me about it. And at the rate I'm paying, I'll still owe for about three years after reaching my life expectancy."

"Then why did you quit?"

"I didn't *quit*," she said in a huff. "I simply believe there is more to medicine than drugs and surgery. There was no room for my way of thinking."

"If your appendix ever ruptures, wouldn't you want a qualified surgeon around?"

"Of course. But if I get a cold, I'd rather treat it with the herbs and teas used by my ancestors."

"I agree on that point."

"I believe in healthy living and prevention. Medical intervention is a last resort for me."

"I do like that honey-lemon thing you make whenever I catch cold."

"A time-tested remedy."

"I like it even better with some bourbon in it."

She slapped his thigh. "Bourbon is not part of my recipe."

"No, just a minor alteration."

Val turned in her seat. He liked the neat way she tucked one leg beneath her. He liked the way her sweatshirt had pulled taught against her body, as well. All the while, Chance was wondering what had gotten into him. Val was important to him. She was a friend, a co-worker. He wasn't supposed to think carnal thoughts about her. But he was.

"Hello?" Val called, snapping him back to reality.

"Sorry, what?"

"How did Seth take the news that Savannah is pregnant?"

"I wasn't there, but I'm sure, knowing Seth, he did a fair share of chest-pounding. Apparently Seth and Sam and Cade went out to celebrate with their wives. They were probably plotting ways to repopulate the world with mini-Landrys."

"You're all used to a big family," Val opined. "I wouldn't know how to function in a family of seven."

"You claw your way to the top," Chance

teased. "Worked for everyone but Shane. He would always get a bruise, go running to Pop, and then the rest of us would get a serious whupping."

"Sounds like it was a real zoo."

He shook his head. "Actually, it was great. You were never at a loss for someone to hang out with. Chandler and I used to ride up into the mountains and camp for a day or two."

"Somehow I don't see you as the outdoorsy type."

Chance purposefully lowered his voice. "Me man. Me make fire."

"You may be man, but I'd bet you probably used matches and propane."

"A lighter, actually," he admitted easily. "I wasn't anything like my father. He could survive for weeks up in the mountains. Shane's like him in that way. I'm more like Chandler."

"Is that because you two are the pretty ones?"

"Handsome," Chance corrected. "But I was smarter. That's why Chandler is only a B.A., so I win."

"I didn't know life was so competitive between the Landry brothers."

"Hell, yes. That's the one thing we all have in common. None of us likes to lose."

"And you consider anchoring the news losing?"

"Read and nod?" he joked.

"I think Chandler is great."

"Really? I guess you've never seen his feet."

"What's wrong with his feet?" Val asked.

"Nothing—if you like webbed toes."

"You're lying," Val returned with a soft chuckle. "I've seen his feet. He has nice feet. No webbing."

"When did you see his feet?"

"At last year's Labor Day picnic. Chandler and I were partners in the three-legged race. We were both barefooted."

"Why'd you pick Chandler? He's the slowest one in the bunch."

"He picked me," Val retorted.

For some reason, that didn't sit too well with Chance. He felt something in the pit of his stomach. He couldn't put a name to it, exactly. He just knew it was uncomfortable and annoying.

"Why the frown?" Val asked.

Chance brushed off her comment as he

pulled the SUV into the parking lot adjacent to his office. "Let's get the supplies."

He was staring intently at his boots when he heard Val's sharp intake of breath. He looked at her and then followed her line of sight.

"What the hell?" he demanded.

Chapter Three

His office door was wide open.

At the same time he killed the engine, Tara, the billing clerk, appeared in the doorway.

"I'm so glad you're here!" Tara gushed. "I've been calling around trying to find you."

"What's the problem?" Chance asked. He didn't need an answer when he stepped inside the waiting area.

"You should be in church on a Sunday morning," Dora Simms managed to chastise through her clenched teeth.

"I found her like this when I went by to drop off her bill from the pharmacy. I do Guy's billing, too, you know. Her account is overdue and so I thought if I delivered the bill personally, I could make some sort of payment arrangements. She was on the floor, curled up in a ball," Tara supplied. "I brought her here. I was just writing you a note when—"

"Let's get you more comfortable, Miss Dora," Chance interrupted.

As if choreographed, Val took one side, he took the other and together they managed to get the frail woman into the examination area.

Chance slipped out while Val helped Dora into a gown. He found his billing clerk lingering behind the desk.

"Will she be okay?" Tara asked. "Should I have driven her to the hospital instead?"

Chance offered the wide-eyed woman a reassuring smile. "I'm sure it's her osteoarthritis. Dora refuses to accept that with age comes limitation."

"I was typing out a note for you," Tara explained.

Chance patted her shoulder. "You did the right thing," he assured her. "How did you get in?" he asked as he began a search for Dora's patient file.

"My key," Tara replied sheepishly. "Remember? You insisted on giving me one so

I could get in to do the billing on weekends or when—"

"Right," Chance agreed. Tara was a sweet girl, but she had a habit of giving lengthy explanations to simple questions. He was making a second pass through the *S* section of the filing system to no avail.

"Here," Tara said, shoving a chart at him from arm's length. "I got her file. I thought you and Val might need it and I know that Val usually does—"

"Thanks," Chance acknowledged, taking the thick folder. "I'd better see to Miss Dora."

Chance walked down the hallway, flipping through to his last note on his patient.

He knocked, then opened the door to the exam room. Dora was hunched over at the end of the table, one calcium-deposit-gnarled hand rubbing the small of her back.

"What were you up to this time, Miss Dora?" he asked with amused accusation.

"Don't be impertinent, Dr. Chance," Dora warned. "I've known you since you were a baby. 'Sides, you should show respect to your elders."

"I respect you, Miss Dora," Chance insisted. He sat on the stool and rolled it over to the table's edge. "I'm sure I'll also respect whatever foolish thing you did. Your spine is almost fused from arthritis, Dora. You've got to accept that and stop exerting yourself like you're twenty. Your muscles can't move the way they used to. So, what were you doing?"

Dora snorted. "None of your business what I was doing. I should have had Tara take me to the hospital. I was there a month or so ago and the doctors over there are nice and compassionate to helpless old women."

Chance laughed. "You are a lot of things, but helpless isn't one of them." Chance began his examination.

"Dammit! Don't do that!" Dora insisted, clearly in pain.

Chance looked over at Val. "It's a muscle strain but let's get an X ray just to be on the safe side."

"An X ray?" Dora repeated. "How much does that cost? Lester didn't leave me much when he died."

Chance was well aware of the fact that Dora Simms, like many of his patients, didn't have private medical insurance. Most folks in

Jasper were self-employed. They often struggled to pay for the necessities, and medical insurance was considered a luxury few could afford.

"Don't worry, Dora," Val said. "I'll see that Tara files the Medicare forms for you."

"She's a strange bird," Dora commented. "I'm grateful that she came by the homestead and found me. Lord knows, I could have been laid out on the floor for some time before anyone noticed, but I wonder about people who won't look you in the eye."

Chance smiled. "She probably thinks you're a cantankerous old woman. I'll bet she's afraid of you. I'm sure she knows that old story about you taking out your shotgun when the guy from the phone company came to collect."

"He deserved to see the business end of my shotgun," Dora insisted. "It wasn't my fault that all those long distance companies tried to cheat me. If you ask me, the phone system hasn't been worth a damn since they broke it up into pieces."

"Let's get your X ray," Val said. "We can debate the divestiture issue later."

Gingerly, Dora got down from the examination table and went with Val into the adjoining room. Chance was still smiling as he made a few notes in the chart. It was good to see Dora full of spunk again. Losing her husband of nearly fifty-one years had been difficult. The last time Chance had seen her was about three months earlier. He'd prescribed a monoamine oxidase for her. He had also suggested she consider some sort of counseling for her depression. Dora told him then that only time would help her. Apparently she had been right.

Chance left the exam room and went to the drug cabinet. He unlocked it and reached around until he found a handful of samples provided by the pharmaceutical company representative.

Val came out into the hallway with a still-wet X ray film between her thumb and forefinger. She thrust it up onto the board and flipped on the light.

Chance went up behind her, his eyes scanning the image for any signs or symptoms that contradicted his diagnosis. He reached up to smooth a corner of the film. In the process, his arm rested against the pulse at base of Val's neck.

Her skin was warm, soft and silky. He was suddenly and keenly aware of her. He breathed in the floral scent. Felt the heat in the scant inches of space that separated her body from his. He knew it would be a simple thing to turn her to him. Then a single step and he would be able to pull her against him. He imagined cupping her face in his hands, tilting her head upwards. Then, he would…

"Have myself committed," Chance muttered, snapping his arm to his side.

Val didn't turn around. "Reading an X ray has caused you to suffer some sort of psychotic break?"

Was her voice always that low and sultry? he wondered.

"Just thinking out loud," Chance replied when he was sure his tone would sound even and controlled.

Val flicked the light switch and pulled the film from the board. She turned, slowly, in his direction. "What do you want to do?"

Something immoral, his conscience replied in silent disgust. "Already done," Chance told her, holding up the drug samples. "A non-steriod antiinflammatory should take the edge off most of the pain. Got any suggestions on how to get her to rest until her back muscles heal?"

Val offered a smile that knotted his gut. "Staple gun her to her bed?"

"I heard that!" Dora called as she shuffled out into the hallway. "I'm old, I'm not deaf."

"No," Chance agreed, "but you are doubled over and unless you give your body time to heal, you'll probably stay that way."

"And just who do you think is going to tend things while I'm laid up?" Dora demanded.

"I'll make you a deal," Val suggested. "I'll send one of the young men from the reservation out to help you for a couple of weeks."

"I can't pay," Dora snapped, not with anger but with a fierce pride that Chance respected.

"For barter," Val countered. "You can give one of your new calves to the tribe and write it off as a tax deduction."

Dora scoffed. "One calf for two weeks' work?"

"Okay," Val countered. "Two weeks of full-time work *and* someone will come by three times a week all summer to help you with the yard and garden."

Dora smiled through her pain. "And they have to bring out my groceries when they come."

"Done," Val agreed.

"Now that we've worked out the terms of your surrender, Miss Dora, get dressed and I'll be right with you."

"I'll help you," Val offered.

"No need," Dora insisted, going into the exam room and slamming the door behind her.

Val went to the computer and sat down. "I need the chart," she told Chance.

He retrieved it from the table next to the drug cabinet and joined Val in the small office area. After glancing at the screen, he asked, "What's that?"

He heard Val's soft chuckle. "Tara's note saying she'll call your son."

"I don't have a son," Chance commented.

"She means *soon*," Val explained. "It's her chronic typo, or didn't you notice that you have a lot of bills that look forward to the 'patient's remittance of a 'son'?"

"I didn't notice," he admitted.

"My chronic typo is 'form' when I mean 'from.'"

"I thought those machines were supposed to catch stuff like that."

Val tossed a chiding glance over her shoulder. "It's a machine. It only knows when you have misspelled a word, not misused it. Give me the script details."

Chance gave her the dosage directions and watched as she navigated her way through what seemed like a maze of different colored screens. If this was progress, he wasn't sure he liked it. It seemed far simpler to just write out a prescription, copy it and hand it to a patient.

"Want me to send this over to Guy's pharmacy?" she asked.

"Wouldn't it be easier to walk it over than to mail it?"

Val shook her head. "Send it as in modem," she explained, clearly amused. "We're interfaced on the same—"

"I'm glazing over," Chance insisted. "I'm going to give her a sample. It will hold her for a couple of hours until Guy can fill the prescription."

"I'll fill out all the forms she needs for Medicare," Val offered. "Guy will fill it in a snap. I'll add a note that she needs it right now. I'd hate for her to have to come back into town just for her medication."

"Thanks, Tara," Chance mumbled. "How delinquent is she at the pharmacy?"

Tara lowered her voice apparently concerned that she might offend the elderly patient. "She says the pills you gave her were to make her happy and she can't be happy if she has to pay ten percent of the cost of the drug."

Chance sighed. "Tell Guy I'll cover her bill for the Nardil. I don't want her depression getting any worse."

His remark earned him a smile from both women.

The printer buzzed to life, spitting out a sheet of paper. Val picked it up and scanned it. "She's all set."

"All set for what?" Chance asked.

"The program automatically alerts if I input a drug that is contraindicated. No contraindication, then it creates an instruction sheet for the patient to follow. See?"

Okay, so it was kind of impressive that the

computer could do so much. But he still wasn't enamored of the thing.

"Sign there," Val said, tapping the line at the bottom of the page.

Chance did as instructed, watched as Val made a copy of the paper for the file, then greeted Dora when she emerged from the exam room.

He explained the medication and handed Dora the sample. "Is your file up-to-date?" he asked. "You need to tell us if you start taking anything new. Even over-the-counter herbs or potions."

Dora's grin quickly turned into a grimace. "No, nothing new. But does bourbon count?"

"Yes," Chance said. "No alcohol while you're on this drug, Miss Dora. C'mon, we'll drive you back home."

They stopped at the pharmacy where Chance discretely paid Dora's outstanding balance and picked up the new medication. Dora complained for the entire ride out to her beleaguered ranch. After much negotiation, Chance and Val did cajole her into bed with a hot water bottle before heading out to the reservation.

It took the better part of an hour before the sign announcing the boundary line of the reservation came into sight. The sign was bent, twisted, and had a few dozen pellet holes from someone or some ones using it as target practice.

The sign itself wasn't really necessary; the surface of the road was indication enough. Relatively smooth blacktop slowly melted into cracked and rutted macadam. Eventually, all traces of surfacing disintegrated, leaving nothing but uneven gravel and dirt.

Val could hear the ding of pebbles hitting the undercarriage of the vehicle. The scent of an open fire wafted in on the breeze. Wildflowers grew along the roadside, sometimes up through the rusted remains of an old, abandoned appliance, car or piece of rusted heavy machinery.

Several dogs ran alongside the car as they neared the edge of a cluster of dilapidated homes.

"Stop at my place," she instructed.

"Your place?" Chance repeated.

Val pointed to the neat, single-story home that was partially obscured by a small crowd.

"Just pull into the driveway."

Val opened the car door and was immediately greeted with gifts. She had several loaves of bread, home-canned foods and some beautiful handcrafts by the time she reached the house.

There was no shortage of volunteers as Chance began to unload the supplies. He was greeted with warm, friendly smiles and a few whispered giggles from the preteen group. It seemed as if there were no end to deeply tanned, weathered hands willing to pitch in.

The house Val had identified as her own wasn't anything like her home in Jasper. What would have been a living room had been converted into an examination area.

"I recognize that cabinet," he commented as he handed her gauze and 4-by-4s.

"One man's trash is another man's treasure," she quipped.

"An old Indian saying?"

"Antiques Roadshow," she returned with a smile. "All it needed was some paint and a new leg."

"You told me it would be easier to get a new one," Chance reminded her.

Val grinned. "It was easier. For me," she clarified with a glint in those amazing eyes.

Chance looked around and spotted several other items that had once, in whole or in part, been in his office. "How long have I been subsidizing your operation?" he asked.

"I think I pilfered my first gross of tongue depressors on my third day." She called to a young man who looked to be somewhere around twenty.

It didn't escape Chance's notice that the young man seemed thrilled to be singled out by Val. He also recognized the poor kid's ill-concealed attempt to appear cool in the presence of an attractive woman.

Val reached into her pocket and gave the kid some cash.

Then, somewhat reluctantly, the kid turned, grabbed a friend of similar age and walked out of the house.

There was a low din of conversation coming from the line beginning to form at the doorway. He continued to assist Val in stocking the shelves, cabinets and tables. He was being helpful. He was doing something good for the community.

Who are you kidding? You aren't thinking about the community. You're thinking about the way her sweatshirt rides up when she reaches for the top shelf. You're thinking about the way her jeans hug the outline of her incredible body. You're thinking that catching just a teasing glimpse now and then is more erotic than anything on earth.

"So, Dr. Landry, ready to do some free exams?"

"You have no idea," he told her, hoping she hadn't noticed the catch in his voice.

Val didn't stop to ask what he meant by his cryptic answer. In fact, she wasn't sure she dared speak at all. Either she had totally gone off the deep end, or she had seen something in Chance's expression that caused her heart to add an extra beat. For a millisecond, she could have sworn those gorgeous eyes of his held just a hint of interest. And *not* the friend kind of interest. Was she seeing something she wanted to see or had Chance suddenly realized she was a woman? *Stop!* her brain insisted. It wasn't like she could lean over and ask him for clarification. She played out the scene in her head.

"Gee, Chance, did I just catch you giving my derriere a lusty glance?"

"No, Val, I don't lust after you, but thanks for asking."

The mere idea of it delivered a shiver full of humiliation. *Focus on work.*

There was no lack of work. For the next three hours, she and Chance saw and treated several infected ear canals, cleaned and cared for neglected lacerations, gave immunizations and updated tetanus shots.

"I made your lunch," a young, pregnant woman said. "You eat first."

"Thanks, Leta," Val said as she accepted the basket. "How are you feeling?" Val passed Chance a sandwich.

"I want this baby out now."

"Not too much longer," Val assured her, placing a hand on the woman's belly. "Still a soccer player, huh?"

"Kicks like a mule," Leta agreed.

"How far along?" Chance asked.

Leta let out a breath and answered, "Three more weeks. I'll give you two time to eat. I'll be back in a few minutes."

Val hopped up on the exam table and dug

an apple out of the basket. "Good?" she asked after he had taken a bite of the sandwich.

Chance peered back, then in a low voice said, "It's missing something."

"What?"

He peeked in between the two slices of bread. "I've never had a BLT without any bacon."

"Shane never complains."

"Shane never complains *to you*," Chance countered. "You don't have to believe me. Ask Taylor. She'll tell you all Shane ever does is whine."

"Taylor can't give an objective opinion," Val said.

"I thought you liked her."

"I do. I just happen to think that Taylor isn't in any position to comment."

"Why?"

"I think she's in love with Shane, but I was under the assumption that it was unrequited."

She saw a conspiratorial glint in his eye.

"Me, too. But don't try and tell Shane that."

"Don't try and tell Taylor that," Val countered. "She has a serious case of denial going on."

"Shane, too."

"It ought to be fun to watch," Val said. "Shane will eventually come around and admit how he feels."

Chance shook his head. "Not gonna happen. Taylor will have to make the first move."

"Care to make a friendly wager?" Val asked.

One dark brow arched high on his forehead. "What are the terms?"

Val shrugged, hoping to think of a decent answer. She was fairly sure that admitting that, win or lose, she'd take a mind-altering kiss as payment or punishment probably wasn't appropriate. "If I'm right and Shane crumbles first, then you agree to help me here one Sunday of every month for a year."

Chance whistled. "A year is a big commitment."

She rolled her eyes. "Six months, then."

He nodded. "What if Taylor breaks?"

"What do you want?"

His smile was deliberate, slow and sexy as hell. "I'll name my terms later."

"Do I look stupid?"

Chance's gaze slowly moved from her face, down her throat, then leisurely down to her feet. It felt nearly as intimate as being touched and her pulse quickened.

"You definitely don't look stupid."

"Do I say *thank you* or slap you?" Val responded hoping levity would be a graceful way out of what was becoming a rather tense moment.

His eyes met hers. "Slap me."

Val swallowed, trying to get her muddled brain to decipher whether he was teasing her or taunting her. She was about to ask when her cell phone chimed to life.

"Hello?"

"You've gotta come now!"

She recognized the harried voice of Paul, one of the young men she had sent to help Dora Simms mere hours earlier. "Calm down. Did you have an accident on the way?" Val asked.

"It isn't me! It's the old lady. She's dead."

Chapter Four

Val seemed to take the news of Dora's passing with quiet anger. Chance knew her well enough to recognize the flame of injustice burning behind her stare. It was a stoic response to a horrible situation. He couldn't believe Dora was dead. Chance pretty much wanted to hit something.

Anything.

Then he saw Benton and the urges in him grew tenfold.

"What the hell happened?" Chance demanded.

"You tell me, Landry. She was in full cardiac arrest when the paramedics arrived on scene."

Chance muffled a curse, pivoted on one heel and allowed his frame to slouch against the cool tiled wall of the hospital corridor.

His brain was racing in dozens of different directions at once. And nothing seemed to be making sense.

"I listened to her heart this morning," he said. "Nothing unusual. Her BP was fine."

Val placed her hand on his arm. It felt warm and comforting.

"She could have ruptured an aorta. Maybe a pulmonary embolism?"

"No signs of coronary problems," Benton injected. "She's on her way to post for full autopsy. The initial tox screen was interesting."

Chance lifted his head and met Benton's level gaze. "And?"

"Positive chemistry. The lab will be able to tell us what was in her system in about an hour. In any event, you're going to have to explain to her family how she could be in your office this morning and you managed to misdiagnose whatever killed her."

To Benton's marginal credit, he had the self-restraint not to look pleased as he predicted the future.

Still, Chance hated the idea that he had missed something. Especially when that something turned out to be fatal.

VAL AND CHANCE had been in the doctor's lounge for one hour and seventeen minutes. Val was pouring him another cup of rancid coffee. They had been over a dozen or so scenarios that could have led to Dora's unexpected death.

"You aren't God, Chance. I'm sure you did everything possible. You aren't a psychic, either," she added with a pat to his hand. "Arteries tear without warning. Hearts stop beating. Blood clots form, and all of those things can happen without a single symptom. Especially in women. How many women have we seen that mistook the warning signs of a heart attack for indigestion? C'mon, Chance."

"It'll be good to get the results of the tox screen."

"Not necessarily," Benton opined, marching into the room like a well-armed invader. His weapon was a multipage printout on the familiar green paper from the pathology lab.

"Her tox screen shows elevated levels of phenelzine and meperidine."

Chance rose and snatched the papers from Benton. Scanning them quickly, he said, "This isn't possible. I prescribed Naprosyn for Dora because I knew about the anti-depressant."

"The lab called the pharmacy. You prescribed meperidine, Dr. Landry. You gave your patient a contraindicated drug that resulted in her death."

"Oh, Lord," Val gasped.

"I did not," Chance insisted, replaying his consultation with Dora in his head. "I know what I prescribed and I was fully aware of Dora's meds."

"The tox screen and the pharmacy disagree, Landry. I'm taking this to administration."

"Blow it out your ear, Benton," Val grumbled, placing herself between the two men. "I know Chance adhered to the highest medical standards."

"Don't worry, Miss Greene, I'm sure you'll have a chance to sing Dr. Landry's praises to a review board." He glared at Chance for an additional second. "I'm going to take this and the incident with Kent Dawson up the ladder. I want your privileges suspended before you kill anyone else." The snooty doctor waltzed away from them.

"The only person I'm even remotely interested in killing is you, Benton!" Chance called after him.

"Relax," Val soothed. Actually, it was part placation and part castigation. "Don't worry about Benton."

"I'm not," Chance sighed, raking his hand through his hair. "I'm wondering what in the hell I'm going to say to Dora's brother Gary."

"You'll think of something," Val promised. "Let's go down to the chapel and talk to him."

"And tell him what?" Chance challenged.

"The truth. We don't know. All you can tell him is that the tests are pending."

"The tox screen isn't."

Val sighed. "The tox screen could be flawed. We'll do another one."

"Right, I'll just mosey down to the path lab and get some blood. I'm sure Benton has told the whole world not to let me anywhere near Dora."

"I can do it," Val offered.

He gave her a weak smile. "Thanks."

Chance went off to do the worst job any doctor must face…telling a family member about a loss.

VAL'S JOB was far more simple. She took the elevator down to the basement and followed the faded yellow stripe painted on the floor through three sets of double doors until she reached the morgue.

The air was thick with the smell of antiseptic and death. It was cool and brightly lit. There were two desks against one wall, both cluttered, neither occupied. There were three tables in the center of the room; luckily, none of them was occupied, either. Val was never fond of the hands-on moments in medical training. She preferred to treat the dead with reverence, not scientific curiosity.

There were various instruments along the walls, some for magnifying samples, others for tissue shaving, still others for specimen collection. This was the necessary and valuable, but unpleasant, side of medicine. Val rubbed her arms as a small shiver ran up her neck. She could close her eyes and remember the sounds and nauseating effect of the bone saw. Dismissing her personal aversion to the room and its purpose, she stepped over to a cart and began opening drawers. In the third one, she found syringes and test tubes.

This was the easy part. The hard part was walking through the polished stainless doors into the cooler. In spite of her years in school, she was afraid in the company of deceased people. Maybe it was too many horror movies as a child. Or perhaps it was her strong belief that there is something after death. At any rate, she wasn't thrilled with the reality of what she had to do.

She walked to the door and gave the handle a pull. It didn't move. She tried again. Still nothing.

Val turned and let out a high shriek as cold fingers gripped her wrist.

"Don't stab me!"

Val swallowed the lump in her throat and stared at the tall lab tech holding on to her. "I—I wasn't going to stab you," she insisted. Then, realizing she had the syringe in her hand, she offered a half smile. "Sorry. I forgot I was holding that."

He let go of her and his eyes searched her face questioningly. "I came to get a blood sample," she explained.

He nodded and grinned.

Val relaxed.

"No can do," he said, then moved and waved his arm toward the door. "You're Val Greene, and I'm not supposed to let you anywhere near the cooler."

"I'm here to perform a medically necessary blood collection."

He shook his head. "Administration called two minutes ago with strict orders that no one was allowed access down here without Dr. Benton in tow or a warrant in hand. Got either of those?"

"No. But I'm—"

"Leaving," he said with finality.

Val felt angry and defeated. She didn't hurry as she left the room. Nope, she strolled and tried to pretend that she didn't care that he had thwarted her efforts.

But she did care. She wanted to know what had happened to Dora and she wanted to prove that Chance hadn't acted negligently.

She walked toward the elevator, near the receptionist who hadn't paid her an ounce of attention then or now.

"...Can pick her up after six tonight," she was saying into the phone. Then a pause, then, "Thank you, Mr. Miller."

Val's spirits brightened. Miller's Funeral Home. She had an idea.

"IT WASN'T your fault," Val insisted as she attempted to place a cold pack against Chance's jaw. He glared up at her with a blend of frustration and unspoken agony clouding his gaze. "Really?" he snapped. "Easy for you to say. You aren't the M.D. with his butt in a sling. I am."

"Your butt isn't in a sling," Val assured him. His stinging comment rankled. "Stop growling at me. I'm on your side, remember?"

"My pal Val," he agreed, though it didn't sound like much of a compliment.

She allowed the ice pack to fall into his lap and wondered why men were such whiners. Had to be in the genes. "Stop pouting like a child. We can get to the bottom of this. There has to be a logical explanation."

He tilted his head to one side. "Really? You're graduating from practicing medicine without a license to practicing law without a license?"

She leveled her gaze on him. "I'm trying

to help a friend. I do that even when the friend is being a self-pitying jerk."

"It isn't your career heading south. Maybe I should have quit before reaching the finish line like you did. Maybe then Dora would still be alive."

Val's fists opened and closed at her sides. But for the fact that Dora's bereft brother had punched Chance at the hospital upon learning of his sister's death, she would gladly have smacked some sense into him. "Does it make you feel better to belittle me for my career decisions? Will it help us figure out what happened to Dora?"

Chance rose and began pacing between the maze of Victorian furnishings. "The hospital is going to do a full M & M. Benton has probably already made a report with the licensing board, the state medical association and probably reported me to the ASPCA just for fun."

"Sit," she commanded, grabbing his arm and gently shoving him back on to the settee. Val took in a deep breath and blew it out slowly as she plunked down beside him. "Put your pity in your pocket and let's start thinking.

And don't," she turned and crooked her finger under his chin, "worry about Benton. Everyone knows that the only way he could get any dumber is if someone cut his head off."

Chance's expression relaxed until there was a faint trace of a lopsided smile. "I like that image."

"Then let's put our brilliant minds together and figure this out," Val suggested.

Chance rubbed his hands over his face. She noted the small creases at his temple that she recognized as fatigue. In all the time she had been with Chance, she had never seen this vein of vulnerability running beneath his easygoing facade. It was almost like looking into the face of a total stranger. A very attractive stranger.

Whoa! her brain screamed. That was definitely from the realm of inappropriate thought. Dora Simms's remains were waiting for autopsy and here she was teetering on the precipice of lust. Not very reassuring to discover she had such a superficial, uncaring crevasse in her moral landscape.

She leapt from the settee as if it was about

to catch fire. Chance noted her skittish, sudden movement, but thankfully didn't comment.

It seemed that the harder she tried to focus her mind on this man's problem, the more her mind kept suggesting that *the man* was the problem. Or more accurately, her wayward musings. Val suddenly felt like a sailboat caught in a storm with a bent rudder and a cracked mast. Her thoughts were going in too many jumbled directions, yet they all seemed determined to head in the direction of her friend.

Friend. She repeated the word in her mind like a mantra.

Focus!

She wasn't sure how to broach the idea that had been born when she'd overheard the morgue receptionist. "Okay," she began as she slipped her shoes off and shoved them under the ornately carved coffee table. "Possibility number one is that the hospital lab screwed up and the results of the tox screen from the E.R. are just wrong."

"They run them twice," Chance countered.

She nodded and shrugged. "Possibility number two is that Dora was taking something else that reacted with the anti-inflammatory or her antidepressant and simply didn't tell you. We both know that patients don't always confess everything at the exam. She could have eaten something or taken any number of over-the-counter things that reacted with one or both of the drugs you prescribed."

"That wouldn't explain why her blood showed a narcotic instead of an anti-inflammatory pain reliever."

"True," Val conceded.

Chance placed the ice pack to his jaw. "Then there is the obvious," he sighed.

"You would not prescribe a contraindicated med to a patient, Chance. You don't make those kinds of mistakes."

"I'm two for two the past couple of weeks," he grumbled. "I'm sure Benton will bring that to the attention of the morbidity and mortality panel."

She glared at him. "Are you sure you want to go with the notion that you've been a wonderful, dedicated doctor for years and in fourteen short days you've done a turnaround and are now a danger to your patients? We both know you are not incompetent, Chance."

"Even you said the order for Kent Dawson's contrast angiogram was probably due to human error. I'm the human who wrote the orders that almost killed him. And I'm the human who treated Dora this morning. Sounds pretty damned incompetent to me."

Val felt her temper begin to simmer. "You are such a…a…man! I am trying to figure out what happened and you're swimming in self-pity and sarcasm."

"I didn't ask for your help, Val."

A crackling moment of silence joined them. Val snatched up her backpack. "Then consider it withdrawn," she shot back. "I'm leaving."

"That's a very *woman* thing to do!" he called after her.

She turned and glowered at him. "What is that supposed to mean?"

"The female solution to things. It's easy for women like you."

"Women like me?" Val rolled her eyes.

"Fine, women in general."

"You're my friend, Chance. You've had a crappy day. We both have. So I'm leaving before I say something cruel and hurtful—

which, by the way, you completely deserve."
She slammed the door on her way out.

"IT ISN'T good," Chance admitted. He was
seated at the kitchen table of the Lucky 7
Ranch, flanked by his brothers Seth and Shane.

"Benton contacted the state police. He
doesn't trust me to investigate because I'm
your brother," Seth said.

"You're the sheriff," Chance countered.
"Can't you arrest Benton for being an ass?"

"Speaking of," Shane whispered as Taylor
came into the kitchen to grab a bottle of water
from the fridge.

"I heard that," she sighed. "You know you
find my derriere amazing, Shane. You can't
help yourself. You're a pig."

Seth and Chance shared a silent chuckle as
the housekeeper sashayed out of the room.

"You're fired," Shane promised.

Chance balanced his chair on the back two
legs, resting his head against the wall of his
childhood home. Once Val had stormed out, he
hadn't felt much like sticking around to be by
himself. Not when it meant being alone with
the fact that he had behaved very, very badly.

"How's Val holding up?" Shane asked.

For some reason Chance found his brother's concern annoying. "Hasn't she come running to you to cry on your shoulder?"

Shane offered one of his irritating baby-of-the-family grins. "If she did, I would do everything in my power to provide her comfort and support." Shane winked.

"Val is off-limits."

The instant the words fell from his mouth, Chance wondered where they had come from.

"Says who?" Shane pressed.

Chance regrouped. "I only meant that she works for me. It would be awkward if you started something with her."

"Awkward for who?" Seth asked.

"Whom," Sam corrected as he strolled in.

Sam fell into the seat on the right side of the rustic pine table. Even now, all these years later, the brothers still gravitated to the seats they had been assigned as children. It didn't matter if one of the Landry brothers had been gone for a year or an hour. The minute they stepped back on Lucky 7 land, things slipped into place.

"I hear there's trouble," Sam commented.

Chance filled his brother in on the situation. "The hospital is going to investigate my entire digestive tract and Benton is leading colostomy."

"Anything I can do?" Sam asked.

"Val and I will have to go back over the records. Assuming she ever speaks to me again."

"She will," Shane assured him.

Chance pointedly ignored Shane as he addressed his other brothers. "The resident expert on my PA. I was a little rough on her this afternoon."

Sam nodded. "I know. She called me when she couldn't get you at the office."

Chance and his brother locked eyes. "You, too?"

Sam shrugged. "Val said you were in a foul mood. She thought you could use some brotherly support."

"Does she have all of you on speed dial?" Chance groused.

Sam shook his head. "She's just worried. She thinks your patient's sudden death is hitting you so hard because you still have," Sam paused, apparently trying to quote from memory, "issues about Mother leaving so abruptly."

Chance felt a cold chill settle inside the pit of his stomach. The mere mention of the family matriarch had a predictable effect on his brothers. Shane stormed off. Seth made some excuse to leave in a hurry and Chance felt his sore jaw clench.

"One psychiatry rotation and she's an expert," Chance commented, his mood dark. "I never made a single mention of our absent mother. So don't even think about rehashing this subject."

Sam held up his palms in surrender. "Don't bite my head off. But you should be able to see where Val is coming from."

Chance scoffed at the idea. "There is no correlation between my mother running off a decade ago and my patient dying from a drug interaction. Val's mad because I was a little rough on her."

"I'd say inferring her abandonment of traditional medicine was akin to quitting and somehow lumping her into a lesser category of women was over the top."

Chance felt a pang of renewed guilt. "I needed to vent."

"Val isn't a whipping post and she really wants to help you get to the bottom of this."

"She might want to consider polishing her résumé," Chance said. "I could be censured or lose my license."

"Then get off your duff and go do something about it. Fix your career situation. That's important. So is Val."

"I know," he admitted.

"So tell her that," Sam suggested. "Don't let what happened a decade ago ruin your life, Chance."

"My potential life-ruination is Dora's death."

"That's career, Chance. Try looking at the big picture for a change. Or do you want to spend your life alone?"

"Don't do that, cat!" she chided as she lifted the animal off her lap. "You have the very bad fortune of being a male and right about now I don't want to be in the presence of anything with testosterone."

The cat glanced over his shoulder and happily walked off with a high flick of his tail. "Great," she grumbled. "I'm getting attitude from a cat now. Definitely not a good day."

Actually, day had turned to night. Val sat at her table, reading Dora's file. Her laptop was on and connected to the office interface. She had managed to build a modest fire in the fireplace to ward off the evening chill. She needed to build a fire in her brain. Spark some sort of hypothesis that would explain Dora's death.

The only embers glowing in her mind were fed by her conflicting emotions where Chance was concerned. She still had some residual anger about his comments. She was also wondering if there was any validity to his impressions of her. She had made the decision to abandon a traditional medical career because she believed there was more to healing than treating the injury. She wanted to treat the whole person. She had never turned away from anything. She had turned toward something.

"I hate you for making me second-guess myself," she muttered as she reread the same note for the third time. "I've made the life I want for myself."

Val stopped and glanced around. "Oh, yes. I'm on the ugly side of thirty. My companion for the evening is a cat I found on the side of the road. I am the epitome of the well-rounded woman. Such a full, happy, fulfilling life."

She went to the coffee pot and poured another cup. "I shall OD on caffeine, solve the mystery of Dora's death and then Chance will have to…"

What? her brain challenged.

Before she could think out the answer, there was a knock at her door.

More out of habit than vanity, Val brushed her hair off her face, straightened her sweatshirt and went to the door.

Part of her wasn't surprised to see Chance perched on her doorstep. But this other part of her came out of nowhere, blindsiding her. He had a bottle of wine in one hand and a huge bouquet of flowers in the other. His handsome face was illuminated by the brilliant moon and his smile was so incredible that she actually felt as if her whole being were made of rubber.

This was not how she was supposed to react to Chance. Her body wasn't supposed to find comfort in the subtle scent of his cologne. Her eyes weren't supposed to notice the reflection of the flames in his gaze. And her heart definitely wasn't supposed to be lodged in her throat.

"I come bearing gifts."

It took her a minute to find a steady voice. "I finally rate the seventy-nine-ninety-nine special, huh? I guess next I'll be learning the secret handshake."

Chance looked puzzled as she accepted the flowers. "What?"

Despite her nervousness, Val led him inside. She went directly to a cabinet and fumbled around for a vase. For the moment, she made a point of keeping her back to him. "This is the floral arrangement you send to women when you dump them. We think of it as something akin to a sorority initiation."

"We?"

"Everyone at the office," she explained. "We know when your woman du jour has outlived her usefulness when you order the $79.99 flowers. We've just always wondered if there was some sort of secret handshake for the I Got Dumped By Chance Club."

"That is really harsh, Val," Chance commented as he came up behind her.

His warm breath caressed the back of her neck. The sensation caused something that was a blend of excitement and womanly curiosity. Val's stomach churned the conflicting emotions, especially when her conscience added a soft dose of reality. Intellectually, she knew that she was Val and he was Chance. They were colleagues and friends. Anything beyond that would destroy both of those relationships.

She prayed he didn't notice the tremble in her hands as she placed the flowers into an undersized vase. Val also prayed that he would place his palms at her waist, gently turning her around.

She would tilt her head back ever so slightly, losing herself in the cool depths of his light eyes. Then, that moment of crackling anticipation would cement them in time. He would reach up and cup her face in his large hands. Slowly and deliberately, his head would dip, until his mouth was a mere whisper against her lips. The kiss would begin tentatively, almost sweetly. But that wouldn't be enough. Val would reach for his head, pulling him to her with a strength born of need and urgency.

With their mouths locked in exploration, Val would be free to run her hands down over his broad shoulders. Feel the corded muscle of his back, then the taper of his waist. Perhaps boldly, she would place her palms against his body and press him to her.

"Did you hurt yourself?" Chance asked.

"Wh-what?"

"You moaned," he replied, reaching for her forearm and turning her palm upward.

Her flush of fantasy quickly morphed into the heat of humiliation. She snapped her hand away. "It was nothing. I'm just not sure this vase is right for these."

"Let's get another one," Chance said, reaching above her to grasp a large crock on the top shelf of the cabinet.

Val clamped her eyes closed. She would not think about the fact that she could feel the entire outline of his body against her. She wouldn't even consider the idea that his cologne engulfed her. Nor would she allow herself to give into her very strong yet irrational desire to turn around, wrap him in her arms and kiss him until the dull ache in her stomach was satisfied.

"Satisfied?" Chance asked once he had placed the flowers in the makeshift vase.

Val knew better than to even open her mouth. She nodded, and then put as much distance between the two of them as possible under the guise of making fresh coffee. *What has gotten into me?*

When she finished her task, she turned to find Chance's eyes boring into her. His brow was furrowed as he asked, "What's up?"

"Nothing," she insisted, hoping it didn't sound too defensive.

He snorted. "Right. You're jumpy and I could feel the tension in your body a minute ago."

Val longed for a giant hole to open beneath her feet so that she could be swallowed into the bowels of the earth. She lowered her eyes, studying her feet, because she knew good and well that she was a lousy liar. Chance knew it too. There had to be some graceful way to get herself out of this awkward situation.

Something short of admitting that she was having a major sexual fantasy about him.

Chapter Five

A troubling thought crept into Chance's mind. "Hey," he began, tentatively grasping her upper arm, "you don't think I could be responsible for what happened to Kent and Dora, do you?"

She shook her head and peered up at him with those incredible eyes. He read uncertainty in the kaleidoscope of color. The notion that Val doubted him was like a hard jab in the gut. Chance allowed his hand to fall away.

"Chance?" Val took his hand in hers. "I know you aren't careless. Why else would I be sitting here hunched over the computer?"

He looked from Val to the computer, then back again. Chance might have noticed the pile of work, perhaps recognized some of the files from the office had he not been so focused on his apology. Technically, he corrected himself, he wasn't focused on his apology so much as he was focused on the softness of her fingertips against the back of his hand. Val was his friend. He wasn't supposed to be thinking of her like this. Maybe it was the stress.

Maybe it was the way the firelight splashed golden highlights in her hair. Or the faint scent of flowers that teased his senses. Worse yet, maybe it was the way his imagination was fixated on the hint of curves beneath soft fabric.

Maybe he needed to get a grip.

"So," he paused to clear the guilty rasp from his voice, "what exactly have you been doing?"

Tugging his hand once before releasing it, Val led him to the table. She tapped once on the touchpad. The screen switched from a LSD-inspired series of wavy lines to the patient roster. She highlighted Dora's file and a new screen popped up.

"This is her entire history," Val explained.

"I don't need a computer to tell me all that," Chance retorted. "I know every ailment, injury and disease the woman ever had."

He heard Val sigh. Her fingers skated across

the keyboard. "You prescribed phenelzine for her three months ago."

"She was depressed," Chance recalled. "I also suggested she see a therapist. As I remember, she told me to go to hell."

Val reached up, took a handful of his shirt, and pulled him down next to the chair next to hers. "Right, you prescribed forty milligrams three times a day."

Chance nodded, reading the same information on the screen. "I don't see the importance."

"And today you prescribed an anti-inflammatory for her pain."

"And?"

Val met his gaze and held it. "Assuming Dora died from a drug interaction, how did she get the meperidine?"

"From Guy's Pharmacy," Chance suggested. "Didn't Benton say he called and the pharmacy confirmed dispensing the wrong prescription?"

"Right," she said. "Which should mean the pharmacy may have screwed up. Not you."

Impulsively, Chance grabbed Val's face and kissed her forehead with a loud smack. He met her eyes and froze in place. His grip softened, morphing from a spontaneous gesture to a contemplative act. A log in the fireplace crackled and exploded, igniting a spark of interest that he could only categorize as carnal. His gaze dropped as her tongue flicked out, adding a sheen to her slightly parted lips. Chance moved his thumb slowly, over the hollow beneath her cheekbone, until he reached her mouth. Gently, softly, he traced her upper lip with the pad of his thumb. He heard and felt her intake of breath. He moved his attention to her lower lip. He made one slow, tentative pass, and then increased the pressure. He repeated the motion, more aggressively as he looked into her eyes. Her expression was a mishmash of emotions. He saw desire—tempered, but it was there. Seeing her response sent a surge through him. That heady, powerful feeling of knowing that he was able to incite a reaction from her.

Never had he dreamed simply touching her mouth would be so erotic. He moved his hand, tilting her head upward slightly. He began to move closer, wanting, almost needing, to kiss her. He felt her breath against his face. It took a few seconds for him to realize she had spoken.

"Don't do it."

Chance reluctantly moved out of his fog of interest. "What?"

Val placed her palms against his chest and leaned back. It was one of the most difficult things she had ever done. But it was the right thing. "Don't kiss me," she repeated, even though she wanted it more than her next breath.

Chance backed off instantly. "Sorry, I thought—"

"You were thinking like a man," Val finished for him, softening the comment with a half smile. "You're having a crisis and, like all men, you assume sex is the appropriate diversion in the midst of crisis."

"That wasn't what I was thinking," he insisted.

She blew out a breath and chuckled. "I know men too well, Chance. And I know you. I won't ruin a friendship because you want a few hours of *not* thinking about your situation."

He tilted his head to one side, studying her until Val thought she would scream in the silence.

"If that's what you think, then you don't know me at all."

She rolled her eyes. "I know you're hurting, Chance. Trying to seduce me won't change that."

He smiled. "I wasn't trying, Val. I was succeeding."

She felt her face burn. "Time was on your side," she grumbled. "But I want us to agree that this was just a momentary lapse."

"Not gonna happen," Chance replied easily, still wearing that annoying grin.

"We're friends and colleagues, Chance. I don't want to lose that."

"Who says we have to?"

Val scoffed. "Your entire adult life. All of your relationships are temporary."

"But mutually fulfilling," he insisted.

"I wouldn't find anything even remotely fulfilling about a brief affair."

"They aren't always brief," Chance offered as a lame defense. "Haven't you ever heard of having fun while it lasts?"

"About as often as you've heard meaningful interpersonal relationship."

"You wound me."

"I will," she promised, "if you don't change the subject. Just accept the fact that I am not interested and let's get back to work."

Chance reached out and brushed her hair away from her face. Her body annoyingly reacted with a small shiver.

"We'll get back to work."

"Thank you."

"But you are interested, Val."

She swatted at his hand. "I am not. Now, can we discuss something constructive?"

Chance retreated to his seat, still grinning but adopting a polite posture. "Absolutely."

"We need a sample of Dora's blood and the dispensing records from Guy's Pharmacy."

"Which we get how?"

She checked her watch. "The blood is simple—a trip to the funeral home, but we'll have to hurry."

"It's the middle of the night. They don't open for hours."

"That's the point," she told him. "I'll change and we can be in and out before anyone notices."

"Why don't we just wait until morning and

call? Besides, we have no way of knowing when Dora's body will be sent to—"

"I know," Val cut in, retelling the conversation she had overheard. Then she sighed. "It isn't like we have any other options. Do you really think Dora's brother will allow us anywhere near her body?"

"Point taken."

"I FEEL LIKE one of Charlie's Angels," Val whispered with amusement.

"Am I Charlie or Bosley?" he asked.

"You're my boost up for now," Val told him, presenting her foot for him to lift her high enough to reach the transom window above the back door. "I never would have pegged you as a *Charlie's Angels* fan."

"Classic jiggle television," he explained as he cupped his hands to create a platform for her foot. "Mandatory viewing for every self-respecting high-school guy."

Val scoffed as she braced herself against the clapboards long enough to pry up the window. Having accomplished that, she retrieved a small flashlight from the pocket of her jeans and pointed the beam into the room below. Once she shimmied through the window, it was about a ten-foot drop to the floor.

"Be careful," he urged. "We don't want to get caught breaking and entering."

"Right now, I just don't want to get caught breaking an ankle," she retorted. "Your concern is touching."

"You want touching?" Chance countered.

Suddenly, his hand was plastered firmly against her bottom. His fingers pressed into the soft flesh and he gave a squeeze before hoisting her higher.

Val didn't need a great deal of urging. She half dove, half fell through the narrow window. It didn't matter that she had hit the hard floor with a dull thud. Nope. Nothing seemed as relevant as the tingling sensation where his hand had been. The imprint of his touch was tattooed on the memory of her skin.

She needed to get her head in the game and out of the gutter. She needed to get the hell off the floor.

Ignoring the fact that Chance was softly, albeit urgently, whispering her name on the other side of the door, Val retrieved her flashlight. The room was quiet except for the low hum of a fan off to one corner. The air was heavy with the scent of flowers. Scanning the room, she spied three large arrangements on tripods against a wall.

Originally a private home, the area she had entered was once a functional mudroom. Now it appeared to be part reception, part storage area. She considered turning on a light, but thought better of it. The place was fairly isolated, but no sense in alerting anyone on the street that she had gained entry after hours.

Val flipped the lock and let Chance into the small area. The brief blast of cool night air seemed to temper the strong floral thickness hanging in the room.

"I think we can now call ourselves criminals," Chance groused. "There's something sadly ironic about this." Chance felt his chest tighten as he thought of his younger brother Clayton. Clayton Landry was currently serving his fourth year of a twelve-year sentence for manslaughter. The family was continuing to work for his release, but thus far, their efforts had been a huge failure.

"Clayton will be exonerated," Val said.

Her small fingers touched his forearm. She had read his mind. Now that he thought about it, Val could do that. She'd been doing it for quite some time. He peered down at her shadowed profile. His brain began a vivid slideshow of memories. Flashes of Val's insights into him played in snippets against his mind. This woman had been a part of his life for years. Not on the periphery, either. Val had been there for every high and low. For weddings, funerals, births, the trial...all of it. She knew everything about him. Well, almost everything. It should have been comforting. Instead, it was down right scary.

"Are you going to move?" she prompted. "Or did you forget that I'm the one who fell on her fanny from the window?"

"You're in good shape," Chance countered, placing his hand against the small of her back.

If thinking about her inside knowledge of his was scary, his next brain trip was a full-fledged nightmare. He felt the gentle slope of her spine beneath the fabric of the worn cotton shirt she'd hastily chosen for their foray into crime. His fingertips dallied just above the waistband of her jeans. If there was ever a moment for inappropriate carnal thoughts, this was it. He recognized it. But couldn't seem to help himself. Chance was totally preoccupied with lusty curiosity. He longed to tug the fabric free from her pants, then slip his hand upward, feel her warm, smooth skin against his palm.

"You're not doing anything," Val chided.

"Thank God for that," he muttered, withdrawing his hand and stuffing it into his pocket.

"What?"

"Forget it." Chance stepped into the triangle of light and reached for the interior door.

It squeaked open, revealing the dimly lit preparation room.

Dora's body was on a table in the center of the room. Yellowish fluorescent light from a long bulb beneath a row of cabinets was sufficient for their task. Val stepped ahead of him, armed with a syringe.

"I'm so sorry, Miss Dora," he heard Val whisper as she quickly procured the sample.

Chance was lounging in the doorway when he heard a noise from the upper level. He cursed softly.

Val scrambled over to him, plastering herself against him as they moved in unison to retrace their steps.

"Now what?" she asked.

"This was your brainchild," he countered. Chance held her against him and backed into the mudroom. He managed to close the interior door soundlessly and then wedged his body between the huge flower arrangements.

He wasn't sure which was more disturbing—knowing that the mortician had returned and would very likely discover that they had broken in and technically defiled a body or that Val would discover the reaction his own body was having to the feel of her pressed against him.

Chance shut his eyes in the dark, insistently willing himself into control. Now was not the right time for him to realize that Val's slender shape fit with his perfectly. Nor should he be thinking about the way her breasts pressed into his chest, more so with each shallow breath. And speaking of breath, he definitely didn't need to be taking notes on the way her breath fell just below his throat, bathing him in moist, warm heat every time she exhaled. Nope. Wrong time. Wrong place.

Hell! He was experiencing all the normal fantasies a normal man was supposed to feel when sandwiched into a tight space with a beautiful woman and a rush of adrenaline. Normally, not a problem. But this wasn't normal. This was Val.

She was holding the vial of blood in one hand. Val suddenly realized that her other hand was flattened against his chest. A well-muscled, rock solid chest. Very masculine. Very manly.

Very wrong!

She was definitely going to burn in hell. What kind of person was she? She was illegally inside the working area of a funeral home and all she seemed focused on was the incredible feel of his body against her own. She felt the warmth emanating from him. Her chin was against his chest and she had an overwhelming urge to turn her head, resting her cheek against him. It would be perfect— she was wrapped in his arms, it would be simple.

It would be crazy! Chance Landry was off-limits. Apparently, it was time to remind her body that she could never be happy with a casual fling with him. She had made that decision within twenty-four hours of meeting the man. Nope, she wanted more from him, she wanted—

"A lobotomy," she muttered as she stiffened and forced herself to listen for sounds of movement.

"A what?" Chance asked in a quiet, rush of air.

Val decided that it was probably better to get caught. At least she could explain what she was doing there and why to Mr. Miller. She sure as hell couldn't admit to Chance that she was lusting after him like some pathetic pile of raging hormones. She definitely preferred taking her chances with Miller. Decision made. Action necessary.

Without preamble, she yanked herself out of the corner, and made a dash for the door.

Chance was on right her heels. He still couldn't believe she had suggested he get a lobotomy. How in the world was he ever going to explain his body's...*rigid* response to her? He played the scene in his mind:

Sorry, Val. I didn't mean to get a serious erection back there. That was sure to smooth things over.

Maybe Miller could just shoot him during their escape.

Chapter Six

"You must be hating me about now," Val said as soon as they had reached the parking area adjacent to the office. Chance had been oddly quiet since their successful escape from detection.

"You were right," Chance commented, slamming the gearshift into Park.

Val felt herself cringe. Any minute hope she might have clung to that her interest had gone unnoticed vaporized. As much as she wanted to slink off into the night, that wasn't the adult thing to do. Besides, it would only delay the inevitable. They had to talk this through. Clear the air. Get things back to normal.

Problem was, Val no longer felt able to define normal. It was like someone had put Vaseline over the lens through which she focused her life. Everything was blurred, muddled.

She got a brief reprieve. She got an envelope, labeled it and placed the vial of ill-gotten blood into the pickup container for the lab. She put a rush on the results, so they would hear something before the end of the day. Which wasn't too far off, she realized. It was well past midnight.

Val followed Chance upstairs to his apartment. Maybe she was just tired—she was only four hours short of an entire day without sleep.

Chance went to the refrigerator and grabbed two beers. She accepted hers, but placed it on one of the dainty coasters without tasting a drop. She didn't need alcohol to further cripple her obviously addled brain. Conversely, Chance downed his in a few long gulps.

Summoning her fortitude, she decided to get it over with—say everything on her mind on one rush of explanation and hope that was the end of it. "I don't want this weirdness between us Chance."

"Good."

So much for saying her piece all at once.

And the discomfort wasn't over yet. He took her hand and tugged her into a sitting position, then joined her on the settee. The small sofa seemed to get even smaller. She was so flustered that she snatched her hand back, only adding to the awkward tension pulled taut between them.

Val couldn't maintain eye contact, so she averted her gaze, focusing instead on the V of tanned flesh exposed just below his throat. Big mistake.

Monumental mistake. And one that brought a heat of self-loathing to her cheeks.

"As I was saying—"

"Suggesting I have a portion of my brain removed was a little harsh," Chance cut in.

"Not you," she corrected as she met his dark, penetrating stare. "Me. Although, now that you mention it, it would be just as effective if you had the memory of my inappropriate reaction surgically extracted."

Chance stroked his chin, trying not to let the amusement he felt show in his expression. This was priceless! Clearing his throat, he asked, "So you're willing to admit that you found yourself attracted to me the minute I put my arms around you?"

Val's color went three shades darker. He watched as she bit down on her bottom lip briefly, while wringing her hands in her lap. Chance relaxed. Or, more accurately, his guilt and discomfort were effectively eradicated by her admission. He should have just told her it was no big deal, admit that he hadn't even picked up on it. But then he'd probably have to tell her the whole truth—that he hadn't exactly picked up on her reaction because he had been struggling with his own fervent reaction. And simply, the memory of how he had felt for those minutes with her in his arms was all his body needed for a repeat performance.

She frowned. "Can I just apologize and put this behind us?"

Chance grinned. He made sure his next movements were slow and deliberate. First, he inched his thigh, just enough so that he felt resistance as his leg pressed against hers. He covered his true intention by shifting against the furniture, angling himself so that they were as close as possible. He was transfixed as Val opened her mouth, then either lost her nerve or her objection.

He felt the strength of her stare. Found himself impressed that her gaze never faltered. He told himself that he was merely interested in proving to himself and to Val that she had as much curiosity about him as he did about her. While he had no desire to make her feel uncomfortable, he was enjoying the knowledge that she wasn't as immune as she always claimed to be.

Lifting his hand, he simply cradled her face. Her reaction was anything but simple. He felt the heat of her skin and the tiny shiver his touch elicited. He heard her small intake of air and felt the rush of breath against his wrist. The lingering scent of flowers clung to her dark hair. His head dipped lower as his eyes fixed on her parted lips. He wanted to taste her more than he wanted his next breath.

Her tongue flicked out, moistening her mouth. He felt a sharp tug in his groin and barely managed to swallow the groan gurgling in his throat. Chance hadn't felt this anxious and this much anticipation since he was a clumsy teenager attempting to seduce the homecoming queen.

His pulse was pounding in his ears as his mouth brushed hers. It wasn't a kiss exactly. More like a tentative contact—an attempt to wrangle his own strong need so that this lasted more than just a few seconds.

The word *this* reverberated through the drumbeat of his heart. This was Val. He stopped, just a whisper away from her mouth. His ego had gotten in the way of reason. Val had never claimed she wasn't interested in him. She had always maintained that she wasn't interested in what he had to offer.

"Don't do this, Chance."

He hardly recognized her voice. There was a vulnerability to her request that worked like a giant bucket of ice. He leaned back, shaking his head in the process.

"I'm sorry," he managed with a weak smile. "It's been a crappy day and you're right, I shouldn't take advantage of you."

"I wasn't exactly much help," she admitted, returning his gesture. "It wasn't the threat of taking advantage of me so much as it would have been taking advantage of my momentary lapse."

Chance leaned back, resting his arm behind her on the back of the settee. It was much nicer when he was touching her with that hand, but he knew it wasn't what he should be doing. But that didn't mean he had to be a complete Boy Scout. "It wasn't momentary."

"What?"

"Your lapse," he clarified. "It lasted a lot longer than a minute. You were hot for me earlier and you're still hot for me."

She gave his arm a quick and pretty impressive punch. "You don't have to be so smug."

He was glad to see her returning to an even keel. "Not smug. Honest."

"I am not hot for you."

"Are too."

She rolled her eyes. "This is a silly conversation. I think you should take me home now."

"It is silly and I'll be glad to take you home as soon as you admit that you are, in fact, hot for me."

Val glared at him. Crossing her arms in front of her, she let out a loud, annoyed breath. "I am not hot for you."

"Actions speak louder than words. And you were like putty in my hands."

"What are you, the *Dictionary of Clichés* all of a sudden?"

Chance laughed. "Just pointing out the obvious."

"I am neither hot nor am I putty. At best, I am responsive solely and only because sex is a biological need and my reaction to you is coded into my DNA, something over which I have absolutely no independent control."

"Very lame, Val."

She shrugged. "That may be, but I'm sticking by it."

He held out his hand as he stood. "One day, you're going to have to admit the truth."

"Today is definitely not that day."

IT WAS A fairly typical spring morning in Montana. Val's breath condensed into a whitish fog as she shrugged into a light coat to ward off the chill. By midmorning, the temperatures would rise and the sun would warm the cool air. It was a beautiful season, one she saw through sleep-deprived eyes. It had been a long night.

She had downed three cups of coffee before setting off for work. She'd be early, but it seemed like a better idea than just sitting at home by herself.

Chance was already at his desk when she arrived. She could hear him on the phone through the closed door to his office. Val flipped on the lights as she weaved through the reception area and past the exam rooms.

Inability to sleep had given her time to ponder. She glanced at the clock, sorry that Guy's Pharmacy didn't open for another ninety-six minutes. Assuming the results from their lab confirmed the hospital's findings, then she was certain the error was with the druggist and not Chance.

She was stocking the second of the two examination rooms when she heard Chance slam out of his office.

"They suspended my privileges at the hospital!"

"What?"

Chance marched into the hallway looking like a warrior on a search-and-destroy mission. "That horse's ass Benton convinced the hospital administrator to suspend my privileges pending an M & M on Dora's death."

Val searched for something comforting to say but the truth was, there was nothing. And she felt her personal sense of injustice kick in. "I'm sure we can clear all this up by the end of the day."

"Really? How?" Chance reached back and half-heartedly slammed his fist against the wall. "This is complete crap."

"I agree," Val assured him. "I think—"

The phone rang and she grabbed it before Chance could share his foul mood with anyone else.

"This is Moe Mackey, Miss Val."

He was a longtime patient. Long enough so that Val recognized his breathing was weak and labored. "What's wrong, Mr. Mackey?"

He described some shortness of breath and a low-grade fever along with the information that he was just coming off a nasty cold. Val instructed him to come in immediately.

"You want me to set up the portable EKG?" she asked Chance when he got off the phone.

Chance nodded. "He's only fifty, but I

think we should err on the side of caution until this blows over."

Val nodded. "I know it will work out. I'm sure if Dora did get the wrong prescription, it was the pharmacist's mistake."

"Not according to the hospital administrator," Chance explained. "He said they had a copy of my script from Guy's and he swears I prescribed the wrong drug. I wish to hell I would have looked at the bottle when we got it filled for her."

Val shrugged. It wasn't as if they could undo the day before.

Nurse Halloway arrived about five minutes before Moe Mackey. She made sure he was comfortable and placed him in the examination room.

"He looks bad," she confided in Val.

"He said he's been sick for a while."

Halloway lowered her voice. "Not Mr. Mackey. Chance. I know what happened yesterday."

"News traveling fast?"

The nurse nodded. "My sister's youngest goes to school with the girl who works the counter at the pharmacy. She said Guy was fit to be tied when it was suggested that he made the mistake that killed poor Dora."

"The operative word is mistake," Val said. "I'm sure Guy wouldn't intentionally do anything to harm anyone, either."

"That's just it," the nurse continued, "Guy swears on a stack that he sent us a red flag e-mail when the prescription came in. Swears Chance acknowledged the drug interaction warning and e-mailed an override."

"That's impossible," Val insisted. "I was with him the entire time."

Halloway's brow arched. "Every second?"

Val thought for a second. "Pretty much. Except when I was helping Dora. Besides, Chance isn't computer-literate enough to communicate in cyberspace."

"Let's see," Halloway said as she went to the keyboard and punched up the interface information. "There it is," she said, tapping the screen.

Val blinked twice. There was an e-mail from the pharmacy and a response from Chance listed in the computer's respective mailboxes. She didn't call up the actual posts because they were password-protected so they couldn't be accessed. Only two people knew the password. She was one. Chance was the other.

Chapter Seven

Chance took a lengthy history from Mr. Mackey, so much so that he could tell the man was getting a little agitated. It made him furious to think that he was altering his patient protocol when he knew full well that he had done nothing to cause Dora's death. Nor had Chance jeopardized Kent Dawson's health by ordering the wrong test.

Well, he couldn't change any of that this instant, so he focused on the long tape of Mr. Mackey's EKG.

There was nothing abnormal about the test. Which didn't seem to jibe with the distress he saw in the man's face. Chance scratched his head, rolling on his stool over to the desk in the examination room. He called Val over the intercom and asked her to come back to the room.

"Excuse me for a moment," Chance asked, stepping into the hallway to intercept Val.

She looked troubled as she appeared from the reception area. There were deep lines in her forehead, the only distraction from her otherwise flawless, exotic face.

"Something else wrong?" he asked.

She shook her head. "Nope. What's up?"

Chance handed her the now-crumpled strip from the EKG machine. "Am I missing something?"

Val's upturned face was the picture of compassion. "Don't start second-guessing yourself, Chance." She held his gaze for a second and then studied the piece of paper. "Looks fine."

Chance nodded. "I know. But Mackey doesn't look right."

She offered an encouraging smile. "You're very good at reading people. If you sense something is wrong, let's get some more tests."

"Expensive tests," he cautioned. "I hate to put the guy through a battery of unnecessary tests when his EKG is clear."

Val rolled her eyes. "This is why I left the study of traditional medicine. Sometimes you have to ignore the science and go with the gut."

It was Chance's turn to roll his eyes. "How is ordering a chest X ray and arterial blood gases ignoring science?"

"It isn't. It's using science to validate the gut feeling that the EKG isn't giving you the whole story."

"Gimme the strip back," Chance said, holding out his hand. Her little pep talk had boosted him back to normal. After winking at her, he watched as she went to help his nurse wrangle a wayward toddler back into the waiting room.

He arranged for Mr. Mackey to go to the radiologist. If that test was clear, he wouldn't bother with blood gases. He had about thirty seconds between the time Mr. Mackey left and the Kessler family descended on him.

It took Chance, Val and his nurse nearly a half an hour to get throat cultures from four of the five Kessler children. The oldest was just seven and more interested in sword fighting with tongue depressors than seeking medical treatment.

"I don't see anything that troubles me, Mrs. Kessler," Chance told the woman.

She smiled apologetically. "I just wanted to make sure," she admitted. "I was watching two of my neighbor's kids and now they've got strep."

"Everything looks fine."

Val came back with the news that the instant test was negative. She gave the mother the standard warning about false negatives and promised to call with the results of the more accurate culture tests the following day. When the family left, Chance blew out an exhausted breath. Mrs. Kessler deserved sainthood. He admired the amount of work involved in parenting all those young children.

"We have a problem," Val whispered.

Chance felt his spirits plummet. "Someone else is critical or worse?"

"Let's go upstairs," he suggested. Once they were alone, he asked, "What's up?"

Val went to his laptop and brought it to life. Chance cringed. "Not another computer lesson."

She shook her head. "Come here."

Chance went and did as instructed. He looked at the screen. "I've got mail?"

"Open this e-mail," she said, tapping a particular entry.

Chance reached into his back pocket, took out his wallet, removed a small piece of paper and leaned down to type in the password. He scanned the message.

Patient taking phenelzine. Meperidine contraindicated. Reconfirm RX with authorization code.

"Why didn't he say something yesterday?" Chance asked. "This isn't the kind of thing you put in an e-mail. Jeez, Val!"

She waved her hands. "It's a built-in safeguard," she explained. "If a doctor orders a drug from an interfaced pharmacy, the computer identifies the problem. Then the pharmacy sends an alert and the prescribing doctor reconfirms the orders."

"A computer glitch killed Dora?"

"Open the next e-mail," she instructed.

He read the next message.

Patient no longer taking Phenelzine. Meperidine specifically authorized. Dispense immediately.

It was followed by Chance's DEA number and five asterisks. "What is this?"

Val sighed. "We've been over this. One password gets you into the mailbox."

Chance retrieved the slip of paper from his wallet. "The second password solves problems," he remembered.

"*This* kind of problem," Val reiterated. "This requires an immediate response and two levels of authentication so that nothing like this can happen."

"It happened," Chance pointed out, utterly frustrated. "At least I can let Dora's brother know what went wrong."

"You don't get it, do you?" Val pressed.

"No."

"I called the tech guy. There is no glitch in the system. The system worked. The prescription went to the pharmacy. The pharmacy flagged the potentially fatal drug interaction based on the patient history. The pharmacy notified you of the problem and you disregarded the warning and authorized the wrong drug."

"Like hell I did!" Chance exploded. "The most I can do on the computer is get my ass kicked at solitaire. I didn't—"

"I know that," Val insisted. "If you had received the e-mail, you would have taken care of it."

"Damn right. But if all this computer crap is correct, who received and answered the e-mail?"

"The techies swear they verified the routing address—"

"In English, Val."

"Basically, an e-mail leaves a footprint on the information highway. The computer guys can check and verify where an e-mail came from, if it was received, if it was opened, basically everything."

"I don't give a damn if they claim to have a videotape of me reading the e-mail. It didn't happen."

He watched as she shoved hair off her face. She looked as frustrated as he felt.

Chance had a thought. "Someone must have hacked into—"

"Nope. I asked them to check. Not a single unauthorized activity on our server. I had them go back three months to when Dora was first prescribed the antidepressant."

"Great! We're technoscrewed."

"I was with you, Chance. And I know you have no computer skills."

"Great, you can testify on my behalf." He turned and paced in the small space. "I'm starting to understand how Clayton must have felt when Victoria took the stand at his trial."

"This isn't like that," Val argued. "You aren't going to be charged with killing Dora. It will never get that far."

"How can you be so sure?"

"Because…because…"

"Right," he muttered, irritated. "Who would ever have believed that lightning could strike my family twice?"

"Stop feeling sorry for yourself, Chance."

"I'm not exactly getting a whole lot of warm fuzzies from you."

"At least I've been trying to do something."

Chance went to the window and glared down at the street. She was, of course, right. He had no business lashing out at Val, who was doing nothing more than trying to help him. Rubbing his eyes, Chance turned and offered her an apologetic smile. "I'm a real jerk."

She hesitated, then smiled. "Very true."

"I appreciate everything you've done thus far and I'm going to need you if I'm going to get through this."

"Yes, you will," she agreed. "I know you didn't send that order and I know my way around the tech guys."

Right, but I need you, his brain countered. Chance wanted to smack his head, try to figure out how that wayward thought had dropped into his consciousness. He did need her for the reasons she stated. He also needed her because she was a good and dear friend. His rationalizations made her sound like a trusted hunting dog. All of this was making him crazy.

"We have to—"

Chance grabbed the telephone, almost relieved that he had something to focus on besides Val.

"You have to get to the hospital," Mrs. Halloway gushed. "Moe Mackey collapsed at the radiologist's office and he's in bad shape."

"You aren't authorized, Dr. Landry."

"Authorize this," Chance shot back to the security guard near the entrance of the E.R., adding a rather impolite gesture.

"That isn't going to help," Val cautioned as she jogged beside him.

"I don't really care at this point," he admitted. "I only care about getting to Mackey."

He peered into the various treatment spaces as he moved briskly down the corridor. He found his patient in the last curtain area on the right.

"Damn it!" he bellowed, grabbing a handful of the curtain in tightly clenched fingers.

"Step out, Dr. Landry," Benton said, not missing a beat of the CPR rhythm he had going.

"What the hell happened?" Chance demanded.

"Your patient was in serious distress when he arrived for his chest X ray. The attending rushed the chest film, and then ordered an EKG."

"I did one this morning at my office."

Benton tossed him a look full of venom. "Then you did it poorly, Chance. The repeat EKG looked like something my kid would do on his Etch-A-Sketch. I can't believe you missed something so obvious."

Chance took one step backward. "Pulmonary embolism."

"Too bad you didn't make that definitive diagnosis a few hours ago. We might have been able to save him."

A nurse stepped in and handed Benton a lab slip.

"How are his gases?" Chance asked.

"Blood oxygen is almost nil."

Val appeared at his side. Chance felt positively helpless as he watched Benton do everything imaginable to save the patient.

It was a valiant but fruitless effort. Moe Mackey was pronounced dead forty-seven minutes later.

Chapter Eight

The office was silent, save for the low murmur of the aria playing on Nurse Halloway's portable radio. Normally, Chance would be frenetically moving between exam rooms, busy with the usual maladies that crop up during the regular cycle of life. Kids needing school physicals, babies with ear infections, elderly patients demanding flu shots before the onslaught.

The phone had been ringing earlier that morning. By ten o'clock, every patient but one had cancelled. Some were kind enough not to make up a lame excuse. If the callers were to be believed, every grandparent in a hundred-mile radius had either taken suddenly ill or died since news of Moe Mackey's death was reported the night before.

Val and his nurse were giving him a wide berth. Only Tara, the mousy billing clerk, bothered to drop by his office door with an offer to get him coffee.

Feeling pretty useless, Chance decided he needed some air. The full impact of the events of the past few days settled in his gut. He slipped out the side door into the warm afternoon. The blue sky was vast and annoying. The sun was just a little too happy for his current spirits.

Downtown Jasper wasn't exactly a bustling metropolis. At midday, it was relatively quiet. He walked toward Main Street, then across to Jasper Park. Chance sat on a bench across from a weathered bronze statue of Jasper Landry, his great-great-grandfather and town founder. Chance said a silent prayer to Dora Simms and Moe Mackey. He was trained as a doctor to accept death. That wasn't enough to overcome the reality of also being human. A lump lodged in his throat as he sat there, pondering the pointless loss of two decent people.

"I'm closing the office," Chance announced as he burst into the reception area.

"What?" It was a chorus of astonished voices that included the nurse, Val and the bookkeeper.

He smiled at the trio of women. "Everyone will get paid. Call Community Hospital. Have Benton get one of the attendings to cover for me."

"Have the assistant chief of staff—who has never liked you, by the way—help? But, Dr. Landry?" Nurse Halloway began.

Chance paused. "Benton will love the little power trip. And I know this is sudden," he explained. "Truth is, no one in Jasper is racing to my door, but just in case there is someone in this county who wants medical attention, I want the service to have a name for them." He turned to find Val looking at him.

Her eyes sparkled with a blend of amusement and something else. It stopped him almost midstride. He met her gaze and felt the sting of disapproval she conveyed course through him. She gave him a withering look that nearly caused him to fall—face-first—tripping over his own foot.

"You can't close the office!" Tara insisted.

Tearing his gaze off Val, Chance glanced at the bookkeeper. She seemed genuinely horrified by his announcement. He found her sentiment sweet, but it didn't alter his thinking.

Val's unspoken opposition was another thing all together. He hated that she could make him question his decision without so much as uttering a word. Not feeling up to a confrontation, he simply went back to his office and closed the door.

Val waited a full twenty minutes after the nurse and bookkeeper had left before heading toward Chance's door. Anger and frustration accompanied her as she shoved her way into his private sanctuary.

Her nails dug painfully into her palms as her hands clenched at her sides. She could absolutely throttle him about now.

"This is so typical of you!"

"What?"

She noted that he kept his eyes averted. *Good!* She was hoping he was feeling a healthy amount of shame and guilt.

"Don't play dumb, Chance. You know full well that you have an annoying habit of hiding from anything that remotely smells like conflict. Two people are dead and your career is on the line."

Chance's eyes flashed immediate and intense anger. He rose, knocking his chair back in the process. "I know two people are dead. If I could wave my hand and bring them back right now, I would."

He moved around the desk and stood mere inches from her. Val did not back down.

"I don't expect you to raise the dead. But I can't believe you are sitting here doing nothing." She quelled the strong urge to grab a fistful of his shirt to slap some sense into him.

His jaw clenched momentarily. The lines in his forehead deepened. His dark eyes were little more than penetrating slits of blackness.

"You're dangerously close to stepping over the line, Val."

She grunted a bit of her irritation. She would have preferred a long, loud primal scream. "What are you going to do, Chance? Fire me? Well, in case you haven't noticed, I'm the one who has been reviewing patient files. I'm the one who contacted the computer people. Not to mention the fact that I'm the one who bruised her hip falling into Miller's Funeral Home to draw blood from a corpse."

"I've said thank you. Breaking and entering was your idea, so what more do you want?"

He was actually yelling at her. She couldn't believe it. "I want you to get off your duff and figure out what is happening here. Benton may only be an assistant chief, but he's such a power-hungry little weasel that we both know he's going to use what happened to Kent, Dora and Moe to screw with your career."

"I can't control Benton!" Chance shot back.

Val's fingernails dug deeper into her own flesh. "Heaven forbid you address a situation you can't control." She flung this at him with incredible sarcasm. "This is your pattern, Chance. The minute anything gets the least bit complicated, you withdraw and wait."

"No, I accept things, Val. I—"

"Let your mommy issues run your life!"

There was a palpable silence following her statement. For a brief instant, Chance looked as if he was the one ready and willing to throw the first punch.

She took a half step back. "Sorry, that was

a little harsh." The apology was sincere, but she made sure her tone didn't convey complete surrender.

"Mommy issues?" he repeated through partially clenched teeth.

"Because of what happened in your family, you apparently decided that the best way to cope with an unpleasant situation was to do nothing. Your entire life is a testament to that philosophy."

His head cocked to one side, his expression bordered on mockery. "You have no idea what you're talking about."

Val sighed just to release some of the frustration strangling her entire body. "Your ability to disassociate emotion from people makes you a great doctor. You don't panic in tough situations and you can explain dire situations with incredible calm. However, you—"

"Don't need to be psychoanalyzed by you."

"Go to hell, Chance. I'm not going to help someone who is too flaming indecisive to help himself."

"I didn't ask for your help."

"Fine."

"Fine."

She slammed his office door on her way out. She slammed the front door on her way out. She slammed her car door as she headed home.

"THAT WAS incredibly stupid," Shane said two hours later as he sat across from his brother at the kitchen table.

"I agree," Taylor offered.

"You're agreeing with me?" Shane asked.

Chance noted the satisfied smirk on his brother's face.

"I have no problem agreeing with you when you're stating the painfully obvious." Taylor cast a punctuating smile that effectively washed the expression from Shane's face. "I'm going to the market. Anyone need anything?"

"No, thanks," Chance answered.

"I'd like—"

"Anyone but you," Taylor cut in. "See you later."

"I'd like to shoot her," Shane muttered when she was gone.

"I know the feeling."

Shane's open hand slapped against the side of Chance's head. "What the hell was that for?"

"Being a jerk. You have no reason to be mad at Val."

Chance blinked. "I told you what she said."

"Yeah. Some cold, hard truth."

"I guess I need to remind you that you're my brother. You're supposed to have my back."

"Which I will do if you're ever in a barroom brawl. But in this case, I'm afraid I'm voting with Val."

"We're having an election?" Sam Landry said as he entered the kitchen. The eldest Landry brother loosened his tie as he dove into the refrigerator for a beer.

"Val told Chance what an idiot he is."

Sam shrugged. He looped his tie over the back rail of the chair, and then joined them at the table. "An idiot about something specific or just a general idiot?"

Chance's gaze moved from brother to brother. "Thanks for the support guys."

Shane took Sam's beer. He brought it to his lips, branding it as his own.

"You are such a child," Sam grunted, going back to the fridge for another bottle.

The kitchen smelled of the roast in the oven. It was a homey kind of smell, thanks to Taylor. It reminded Chance of the way the house smelled when he was growing up; there had always been something in the oven. Sweet or savory scents wafting through the house from morning until night. He ran through some of his more pleasant memories while Shane filled Sam in on the details of his scene with Val.

Sam wasted no time rendering his verdict. "She got it right."

"How can you say that?" Chance challenged.

"You're a great guy, Chance, and we're all proud of you. Being a doctor and all."

"The doctor part is circling the drain right now," Shane added.

"We should have drowned you at birth," Sam told his younger sibling. "Val's got a point, Chance."

Earlier, Chance had opted not to drink. He changed his mind and got himself a beer. Returning to his seat he asked, "Do you all really see me that way?"

"Yes." They answered in unison.

Chance felt his shoulders slouch. "I disagree. Besides, it isn't like I asked Val to do anything for me."

"You sure as hell aren't doing anything for yourself," Sam said.

"I'm not a wimp!"

"We aren't saying that. Shane and I—hell, all of us—know how tough you took Mom leaving."

"Why is everything always about the mother? Why do laypeople insist on assigning every character trait to the actions of the mother?"

"In your case, it's true," Sam reluctantly insisted. "What happened affected you more than the rest of us. I don't know why. It doesn't really matter. Somewhere along the line, you decided it was easier to back off any tough situation."

"I'm a doctor. I deal with tough situations every other day."

"True. But we're talking about emotional situations, Chance. Face it, anytime anyone or anything gets too close, you cut and run. Which, if you think about it, is exactly what Mom did."

"I don't want to think about it," he admitted. But something in his brother's words rang true. His personal history was an illustration of emotional distance. He avoided complications. Until now. He couldn't avoid the grim reality that two of his patients had died.

"I've got to go."

"Running away?" Sam inquired evenly.

"Nope. This time, I'm running toward something."

Chapter Nine

Guy's Pharmacy was housed in one of the oldest buildings on Main Street. It faced Jasper Park and was a mere two blocks from Chance's office.

After carefully angling his SUV into a parking spot, he sat for a minute, going over the procedures Val had told him.

Guy was a fourth-generation pharmacist and the shop had changed little in the more than a century of its existence. There were only three aisles that divided the shop from front to back. A full array of merchandise was available, though quantity was limited by shelf space. Guy was behind the long counter in the rear of the store, his body obscured by several point-of-purchase displays.

Guy was in his early fifties, but his lack of hair added another decade to his age. The fruity scent of trendy shower gels mixed unsuccessfully with the aroma of stale coffee. Guy offered him a smile that was part welcoming, part sympathy card.

"Evening, Dr. Landry. I was just about to close up."

"Sorry about that," Chance said, extending his hand to the shorter man.

Guy had to lean forward to reach across the counter. "I guess you're here about Dora?"

Chance nodded. "I'd really like to get to the bottom of this. Unfortunately, I'm not the most knowledgeable when it comes to our computer interface."

Stepping around, Guy opened a hinged half door and motioned Chance back into the work area. The place was as neat as a pin. The hand-hewn shelving and counter were at odds with the modern computer equipment. It was as if the bridge of the *Enterprise* fell into The Mercantile from *Little House on the Prairie*.

"I know what you mean about the technology. It took me months just to figure out how to load paper in the machine without jamming it."

"Miss the good old days of prescription pads?"

Guy laughed. "The paper, yes. The handwriting, no."

After rolling a stool into position, Guy turned and wiggled the mouse tethered to the machine and the screen came to life. He started pointing and clicking and highlighting until the machine spit out three sheets of crisply printed paper. He handed them to Chance.

"I swear I didn't override this contraindication warning," Chance said.

"It seemed odd to me at the time," Guy admitted. "I should have asked you about it again when you came by to pick it up. I just assumed that since you were with Dora, you knew about—"

"And I should have read the bottle when I picked it up," Chance interrupted, trying to assuage the man's obvious guilt. "I'm always telling people to check their prescriptions. I should have heeded my own advice."

"Poor Dora," Guy mused, sadness in his

voice. "I still can't believe she's gone. Services are tomorrow. Are you going?"

Chance felt one brow lift as he looked at the other man. "I think her family would prefer I stayed away."

"No one thinks you did anything on purpose."

Chance bit back the desire to state his innocence. And the desire to contradict the man. His patients were canceling left and right. Apparently, everyone thought he was incompetent. Everyone but Val.

He shook his head, a little frightened that her name came to him with such ease. And it wasn't just her name. It was the feeling he got when he thought about her. It was a ball of emotions, all confused and intermingled. He felt guilty for the way he had spoken to her earlier in the day. There was some residual anger over her blunt assessment of him, but that was tempered by his newfound understanding that, like it or not, she was right about certain things.

Then there was that other group of feelings. The ones he didn't want to acknowledge. The ones hinting that on many levels, she wasn't just someone he worked with. If he just lusted after her, that would be fine. Lust he understood. He liked lust. Lust was good.

He left the pharmacy without any new information. Well, he did learn one thing. It was a lot easier thinking with his brain than listening to the first whispers of his heart.

AS IF THE DAY hadn't sucked from start to finish, Val was sure she was getting the flu.

She had lain down on the couch, exhausted after her emotional scene with Chance. Judging from the absolute blackness, that was hours earlier. She leaned up to turn on a light and was painfully blinded by the brightness. Her head felt like someone was banging a cast-iron pot against her brain. She tried to sit, but was crushed by a sudden wave of nausea, cresting over a full-body-tingling dizziness.

She fell back against the sofa. Her vision was blurred, to the point of visual hallucination. She thought she saw someone standing in the window. All she could make out was a dark, hooded sweatshirt and the form of a human being. Beyond that, there was only a fading silhouette.

It seemed like hours until she felt herself move again. Not really move so much as float. She opened her mouth to speak—a feat that seemed to take extraordinary skill and effort. Instead, she coughed. Hard and deep and it felt like she was going to choke up a lung.

Suddenly, she was cold. Then, just as suddenly, she heard the muffled sound of a familiar voice being drowned out by the urgent wail of a siren.

Val felt as if she was caught in a psychedelic sixties film. Sounds seemed to drip colors: reds, blues, bright white. Everything seemed to happen a half second before it registered in her brain.

Through sheer will, she was able to open her eyes. Pain from the light and sound magnified. Everything—including each individual hair follicle—hurt.

She blinked. His face came into focus. She blinked again, not trusting her eyes.

"I need oxygen!" Chance called, but his eyes remained fixed on her.

She started to move, trying to remember how and where her arms were connected to her body.

"Stay still," he insisted. His fingers went to the side of her neck. "You've got a decent pulse."

On the second attempt, she was able to lift her hand to press her palm against his chest. He was holding her. Somehow she was cradled against him, her torso resting in his lap, her head supported by his hand. His heart was pounding faster than the throbbing in her ears.

A flurry of activity erupted around her. An EMT appeared with a portable tank and Chance strapped a mask over her face. She breathed in the antiseptic stream of oxygen.

"Slow and steady," Chance instructed.

Val moved her hand and tried to yank the mask from her mouth. His hand clamped over hers, securing the device. "Wh-what?" she tried to speak.

"Hush. Just breathe."

Realizing that with each breath her headache diminished, Val readily complied. As she did, a parade of firefighters traipsed across her lawn. Chance's broad chest allowed her only a limited view of her house. She didn't see any fire, nor did she smell smoke. Still, she couldn't seem to fit the pieces of memory together to explain how she got out onto the lawn.

Emergency lights strobed as she rehabilitated herself. The sirens had been silenced, but the crackle of staticy radios seemed constant. When she was finally able to sit up, she found herself surrounded by people and supported by Chance. She wasn't sure which one made her more uncomfortable.

Feeling about eighty percent better, she pulled off the oxygen mask and sucked in a stream of cool night air. "What the hell happened?"

"Gas leak," Chance said. "Load her in the ambulance so she can—"

"No ambulance," Val protested.

"Yes, ambulance," Chance insisted. "You need your CO levels diagnosed and monitored."

"I'm feeling better. A gas leak?"

Seth was standing just behind Chance. He looked more like a concerned friend than the town sheriff. To his left, a deputy she recognized but couldn't name was poised, pen and pad in hand.

"You're lucky Chance came by," Seth told her. "A little while longer and I'd hate to think of the outcome."

"There's nothing to leak gas!" she insisted. "I've got an electric stove and I turned the heat off a few days ago."

"It's from the space heater in your kitchen," Chance said. He offered another small smile. "Another thing you appropriated from the office, I take it."

She shook her head. "I didn't take it. I don't know what it's doing here."

Chance took one arm, Seth the other and she stood on fairly stable legs. She went to Chance's SUV and sat sideways on the passenger seat. Seth, the deputy and Chance were all looking at her as if she might magically change colors.

"I don't care that you took the thing, Val. I'm just glad I got here when I did."

"I am, too, but I'm telling you, I have no idea how that thing got into my house."

"Carbon monoxide poisoning can leave you confused," Chance explained, more for the benefit of the two officers flanking him.

Val rubbed her face and then brushed the

hair away from her forehead. Had she taken the heater from the office and—*no!* "I came home, made some tea and lay on the sofa with my cat." She paused and looked toward the house. "My cat was in—"

"Don't worry about the cat."

She refocused. "I fell asleep. I saw—" She paused, trying to clarify the jumble of thoughts in her brain. She looked up at Chance. He was wearing a dark sweatshirt and jeans. "Were you at the window?"

He nodded. "When I didn't get an answer, I looked inside and saw you on the couch."

It seemed as if hours separated seeing him at the window and being carried out of the house.

"The second time."

Val and everyone else turned toward the voice. It was Mr. Erickson, her neighbor. More accurately, his house was a half mile away and angled on the diagonal from the street.

"Excuse me?" Seth said. The deputy began writing as her neighbor provided his personal information, then recapped what he had seen.

"It was just after dinner. I saw your truck." The last statement was directed at Chance. "I know your SUV, Dr. Landry. I pass your office every day on my way into town."

"It wasn't mine," Chance insisted. "Are you sure it was a black Grand Cherokee?"

"Same striping details," he explained. "Coulda sworn it was yours. Anyway, I was watching TV a little while ago when I saw the SUV again. A few minutes later, all the commotion started."

"It wasn't my SUV!" Chance insisted, trying to stem his anger.

"It doesn't matter," Val told him, reaching for his arm.

He looked down and saw the fatigue in her eyes and felt like a fool for bickering over something so inconsequential. "You're right." He patted her hand. "I'm taking you to the office."

"For what?" she demanded.

"Observation. Argue with me and I'll personally put you in that ambulance and sit on you all the way to the hospital."

"It will take hours for your house to air out," Seth added.

That was true enough. "Fine. What about the cat?"

"Bring him by my place," Mr. Erickson offered. "He spends half his life there anyway."

Val gave him a guilty smile. It was true enough. The cat came and went as he pleased. At least, now she knew where he went. "Thanks."

"Anything you want from inside?" Chance asked.

One of the firefighters went in and got her a change of clothing and some toiletries. Seth promised to call them later as he waved them out of the driveway.

"You scared the crap outta me," Chance stated when they turned toward town.

"It wasn't exactly a great evening for me, either," Val teased. "I've appropriated a lot of things for the reservation, but I swear I didn't take the space heater."

Chance simply shrugged. Except there wasn't anything simple about it. Even in the dim glow from the dashboard controls, Val could easily follow the outline of his muscled torso. She swallowed those thoughts. Apparently, her brain wasn't working at full capacity yet.

"It doesn't matter."

"Yes, it does. I don't want you to think I'd steal something from you for my personal use."

He chuckled. It was a low, sensual sound that wrapped around her like an embrace.

"I'm still mad at you," she said more for herself than for him.

"You can't be mad at me. I just saved your life."

"Thank you for that. But the two aren't mutually exclusive."

"Sure they are," he countered easily. One hand left the steering wheel and rested on top of her knee.

The fabric of her jeans suddenly felt thin and transparent. His fingers gently squeezed her thigh. Val didn't know whether to move his hand away or move it to a more interesting location on her leg.

"I really need to be mad at you." *Did I say that out loud?* She cringed and turned her face away from him. "I mean, I'm still really pissed at your behavior."

"Really?"

His fingers moved fractionally higher.

"Of course. You have to stop sitting back and waiting for the next shoe to drop." Words were falling from her mouth at a hormone-high pitch.

"I see."

His fingers were on her midthigh and his thumb brushed back and forth in a silent rhythm. The feel of his hand on her was almost more dizzying than the effects of the toxic fumes.

Worse, when she cast a quick glance in his direction, she found him completely at ease. Her whole body targeted the sensation of his touch and apparently it was nothing more than an absent action for him.

Lord! He probably didn't even realize what he was doing. Val sure did. Yep. She was stunningly aware of the slightest thing—the weight of his hand, the splay of his fingers. How could something so benign have such an impact on her senses? It just wasn't fair.

"Stop it!"

She wasn't quite sure which was worse—the fact that she had snapped or the fact that she had slapped his hand away. The real answer was neither. The worst thing was Chance's smile.

"Your hand was irritating me."

"Was not. It was arousing you."

"Is there room in this car for you, me and your incredible ego?"

He made a production out of resting his hand on the console between them. Val looked down at it as if it were a snake about to strike.

"It isn't ego if I'm stating the obvious."

"The obvious is that I don't want you to touch me."

"Yes, you do," Chance countered with ease as he pulled into the parking lot adjacent to his house.

"Did you have arrogance for dinner?"

He didn't answer. Instead, Chance reached across her for the door handle. In the process, his forearm brushed against her stomach. The contact gave her such a jolt that she almost dove through the window.

Other than the tiniest of headaches, Val felt no residual effects from her encounter with the silent, deadly gas. But then, she was virtually incapable of feeling much more than an acute awareness of Chance. Even the most simple, courteous gesture was imprinted on her brain. She felt his hand splayed at her back as he guided her upstairs. And the inviting scent of his cologne. She could hear the brush of denim against denim as he walked.

"Hungry?"

Val dipped her head and bit her lip. She was uncharacteristically hungry. Overwhelmingly hungry. Pretty much starved.

But not for food.

Chapter Ten

The room seemed to grow smaller with each electric second. Val tried to concentrate on her breathing. She needed slow, calming breaths. Anything that might turn down the fire under her libido. She hoped sucking in carbon monoxide for a few hours was to blame for her inappropriate stirrings. That was a much better explanation than admitting that she would enjoy tackling him to the ground and ripping his clothes off. *Get your brain out of the gutter!*

"I'm really not in the mood to eat."

Chance turned and regarded her with concern in his gaze. "Nauseous?"

Sex-deprived. "No. But I'll take some tea, if you have any."

He rooted around in the cabinets for a moment, and then held up a neatly wrapped package as if it were some sort of trophy. "You should thank me for having the foresight to take this from the last hotel I stayed in." He tossed her the cellophane-wrapped sleeve of herbal and fruited teas, then filled a mug with water and placed it into the microwave. Chance grabbed a beer for himself.

"You should probably sit down."

Val tried to don an air of casualness as she went to the settee. After selecting a cranberry blend from the assortment, she placed the rest on the table. Noticing the printouts from Guy's Pharmacy, she picked them up and read them.

"Who got these for you?"

She looked up to find Chance frowning as he flipped the top off his beer and tossed the opener on the kitchen table. "I put on my shoes and socks and got them myself."

Val was impressed. "You went to see Guy?"

He nodded, then told her about his visit with the pharmacist. The microwave beeped. He brought the mug of steaming water to her, then joined her on the settee.

His weight caused her to slip closer to him

than she might have liked, but there was no way she could move without calling attention to her own discomfort. She would just have to pretend that she wasn't the least bit fazed by his nearness.

"He pretty much confirmed what we already know," Chance explained. "I also got a call from the lab. The blood we sent confirmed that Dora did die as a result of the drug interaction."

"Damn," Val murmured. "I was hoping there was some other explanation."

"Me, too," Chance agreed, his voice laced with sadness. "It's tough enough when someone dies in general, but to die of something preventable…" His voice trailed off.

"At least we know for sure what killed her."

His mood changed, becoming more energized. "But we don't know why."

"Antidepressants and muscle relaxants in those dosages cause respiratory failure from CNS suppression?" she suggested.

"Not that *why*. Why Dora? Why now?"

"I don't follow," she admitted, dunking her teabag then leaving it to steep.

"She was murdered."

Gaping at him, Val wasn't following his logic at all.

Chance shifted, so that he sat leaning toward her. One arm was draped over the back of the settee. The other hand came up and he tucked several strands of hair behind her ear. It was a struggle for Val to stay focused on the conversation and not on the lingering memory of his touch against her lobe. The room was beginning to feel warm.

"You didn't intentionally kill her, Chance."

His grunt of laughter was without humor. "I didn't mean *me*. I *know* I didn't kill her. But someone did. Somehow, some way, someone hacked in and fooled around with the system so that she intentionally got the wrong drug."

"Who would want to kill Dora?" Val asked, her brain kicking into high gear. "And how on earth would someone know that she would need a pain reliever?"

Sighing, Chance let out a slow breath. "I haven't figured that part out yet. But it is the only explanation that makes sense."

"I suppose, in an it-really-doesn't-make-sense kind of way." She was surprised that her lack of enthusiasm seemed to have such a deflating effect on him. "I agree with the idea that this could be intentional."

"Yeah, I'm feeling the confidence exuding from you."

Val took his hand and gave it a squeeze. "I'm not trying to burst your bubble, Chance. Really."

His expression grew serious. There was vulnerability in his eyes that stabbed directly into her core.

"I have to find out what happened, Val. I need help to do it."

She smiled at him and tried to inject some lightness into the intensity thickening the air. "When have I not helped you, Chance? That's what friends are for."

Quietly, he studied her. It went on long enough for her to feel uncomfortable. The heat of a flush warmed her cheeks and a building sense of urgent anticipation gripped her.

His head tilted to one side and it seemed as if he were looking at her for the very first time. Quietly, his gaze searched her face, locking on her eyes, her cheeks and then her mouth.

Val was afraid to move, but more afraid not to.

"I need you."

It was a whisper. An admission that got lost when she felt his lips tentatively brush hers. It was a soft, cautious exploration. One hand moved to her back, the other found the slope of her neck. Ever so gently, Chance angled her head and deepened the kiss.

Indecision evaporated under the enjoyable sensation of his warm mouth on hers. She banished that little voice of reason and allowed her palms to flatten against the solid muscle of his torso. She felt his heartbeat. Traced the edge of his collarbone with the tip of her finger.

The warning cries of her intelligent subconscious faded beneath the surge of desire screaming out from every cell in her body.

When his tongue tentatively touched her lower lip, Val's hands clenched involuntarily. She clung to the fistfuls of his shirt, feeling herself come to life when his fingers glided along her neck, then weaved into her hair.

Somewhere along the line, her role became that of aggressor. Opening her mouth, she returned the kiss with an enthusiasm born of need. He tasted of coffee and mint. His grip on her hair tightened. So did the knot of desire in her stomach.

Slipping her arms up around his neck, she pressed herself against him. It felt as if she couldn't get close enough. When she moved slightly, she heard and tasted the moan in his mouth. It gave her a heady sense of power, knowing that she could have such an effect on him.

Val tested her power. Arching her back, she moved against him. His kiss was no longer tentative. It was a consuming, passionate act. Val nearly cried out.

Chance drew his thumb down her spine. He wondered if she had any idea how sensual she was. Though he had fantasized a time or two about her, he had never dreamed she would taste so sweet. He was amazed by the ferocity of her response. On some level he had assumed she would reject him. On another level, he supposed there was a chance that she would politely allow him this transgression, then allow it to pass. But he had never counted on this. This was incredible. Instead of satisfying his urge, the feel of her tongue sparring with his own created a more powerful need. He wanted her. Now and naked.

Chance pulled away, keeping his hands on her shoulders. The internal struggle over his next action waged hotly in his gut. All of his instincts called to him at once. Especially when he peered into her half-closed eyes and saw her tussled hair. She simply looked like desire personified. His body ached, but not as much as his conscience.

"I'm sorry," he muttered. "I didn't think—"

"Neither did I," Val agreed with a surprisingly wicked smile. "Funny how a person's sex drive can obliterate their brain."

He was stunned. She should have slapped him or flung recriminations at him. He even could have handled her asking him not to stop. But this—she seemed completely comfortable with the mind-shattering moment they had just shared. That was not fair.

Letting his hands fall awkwardly into his lap, Chance regarded her with total confusion. Which seemed to be amusing the hell out of Val.

"We probably should never have done that."

"I believe I pointed that out to you before," she replied, then calmly lifted her mug for a sip of tea. There wasn't even a hint of hostility in her words.

Chance grabbed his beer and took a long swallow. "Don't you want to tell me I was just using sex to solve a crisis? Or that I was out of line? Or—"

She laughed at him. Val wasn't quite sure where the serenity had come from, but she wasn't about to look a gift horse in the mouth. Especially not when her mouth was still warm from the memory of his kiss. "You're sputtering, Chance."

"I'm not sure what to make of this."

"I don't think a federal case is necessary," she teased. "We've both been on an emotional roller-coaster these past few days. I almost died tonight. I'm sure that's why it happened."

Confusion morphed into annoyance. "That may be why we kissed, but it sure doesn't explain your reaction."

"What does that mean?"

"There's a difference between a kiss and a *bone-melting* kiss."

"I can't believe you're shocked. Jeez,

Chance, thanks. I'm glad you've always thought kissing me would be amazingly *average*."

"I never said average," he admitted, clearly flustered. "I just didn't think you would…that you…"

Playfully, she feigned a punch to his arm. "Newsflash, Chance. I've been kissed a few times before."

"But I didn't think you would, well…"

Val rolled her eyes and went to the sink to deposit her teabag. "Then shame on you for not thinking it through, Chance." Spinning, she faced him, but remained in the small kitchen area. "In case you're wondering, I've always thought you'd be an exceptional kisser." She truly enjoyed watching the stain of color appear on his cheeks.

"Th-thanks."

"Can we get back to your theory about Dora?"

Chance swallowed the remainder of his beer. "I'm all for a change of subject."

"If Dora was intentionally murdered, what about Kent Dawson and Moe Mackey? You think someone wanted to hurt them, too?"

Chance's brow furrowed. "Maybe. I'm sure I didn't write orders for the wrong test on Kent."

Val rejoined him, careful to keep a small amount of distance between them. While she was very happy with the way she had handled things, she wasn't quite sure she could muster continued coolness a second time. "Your signature was on the order."

"That's a problem," he admitted. "I sign a lot of things, Val. Maybe I signed it by accident."

"But again, I come back to, if Kent and Dora had enemies, how would they know their confidential medical situations?"

"Maybe we had a break-in and didn't know it."

Val dismissed that idea. "This place is alarmed to the hilt. You're almost always here and when you're not, I'm here or the nurse is here or sometimes Tara." She watched as the possibilities played across his face. "C'mon, Chance. Assuming you never considered me a suspect, what reason could Nurse Halloway or Tara Bishop have for harming your patients?"

"Since I inherited Nurse Halloway from Doc Gibbs, I guess we can rule her out."

"Tara, too," Val insisted. "She's harmless and she does the billing for half the businesses in Jasper."

"She hardly fits the mold of serial killer," Chance agreed. "Tara liked Dora and, as far as I know, she didn't know Kent Dawson other than to say hello. But someone wanted Dora and Kent dead."

"What about Moe Mackey?" Val asked.

"You and I both know a pulmonary embolism can come on quickly."

"True. But his EKG should have shown something."

"But it didn't. Maybe Moe's death was simply a tragic consequence. We know Dora's death was deliberate. Kent's near-fatal reaction was, too."

"So here's what I think we should do—"

"Find out if either of them had any enemies. I can ask Seth to check for any history with the law."

"We've got to get our hands on that order in Kent Dawson's hospital file."

"Why? I glanced at my signature. It was mine."

Val hesitated. "The order was written here.

A copy went into the file here, Kent took one copy and the hospital's computer gets one directly from the interface. What we need is all three. To compare."

"Smart lady," Chance said with a smile that cost her a heartbeat. "Pretty, too."

Val was spared a response by the sound of Seth Landry bounding up the stairs.

"We have a problem," he said without preamble.

"My cat?" Val asked, reading the concern twisting his features. "Did he die from the gas?"

Seth shook his head. "The space heater," he explained.

"You don't need to arrest her, bro," Chance said. "I'm not pressing charges."

"The space heater was rigged."

All humor drained from the room.

Chapter Eleven

Val was only partially aware of the fact that Chance was behind her, his hands protectively grasping her shoulders as Seth repeated the shocking statement.

"The heater's main valve was removed. The heating coil was disconnected."

"Couldn't that have been from an accident?" Chance asked. "We used that heater in the waiting area during the winter. It often got knocked over."

Seth shook his head. "There are tool marks where the valve used to be and the heating coil connectors were snapped by pliers. I sent the thing to the state lab for fingerprints."

Val was stunned. "Why would someone do that?"

"I don't know, Val. But that's not the only bad news."

"Something worse than knowing someone tried to kill her?"

"Not worse. The idiot deputy on the scene with me this morning has a cousin on the state force."

"Why is that bad?" Val asked. "Maybe he can get his cousin to help figure out who did this."

"It's bad because he told his cousin what your neighbor said. The state police think Chance put that heater in your house and tried to kill you."

A strangled sound choked up in her throat. "That's ridiculous! No one would think for a minute that Chance would hurt me. Or anyone else, for that matter."

Seth appeared truly pained. "Chance has the assistant chief of staff at Community Hospital claiming he's intentionally harming his patients. Two have died. The state police have spoken to Nancy Halloway and Tara Bishop. Your nurse admitted to their investigator that the two of you had a pretty bad fight this morning."

"We have fights," Val confirmed. "Your brother can be an annoying jerk at times."

"Tara Bishop refused to confirm the nurse's account, which is the only reason you haven't been picked up for questioning."

"Picked up?" Chance repeated. "I can't believe my nurse thinks I would actually harm Val."

"She doesn't," Seth assured him. "I spoke to her and she feels horrible. She said it was nothing out of the ordinary, that the investigator twisted her words. You're lucky the Bishop woman refused to get involved."

"I'll send her flowers," Chance commented. "Would it help if we went to the state investigator?"

"Absolutely not," Seth stated emphatically. "Benton has poisoned them big time. Did you kill the guy's dog or something?"

"I slept with his wife," Chance answered.

"Great." Seth looked as if he wanted to punch his younger brother.

Val stepped forward and said, "She wasn't his wife then. It was years ago. Benton should grow up."

"How do you know that?" Chance asked.

"I arranged the kiss-off bouquet. She didn't take your rejection too well."

She saw the light of possibility flash in Chance's eyes.

"She was a nurse, right?"

Val nodded. "She worked at Community until late last year. She quit after her second child was born."

"How do you know all of this?"

"I'm social, Chance. People like me."

"I didn't mean to imply that you weren't," he countered. "I'm just surprised that you know all the town gossip."

"Gossip has no basis in fact," she explained. "Everything I just told you is factual."

"What was her name? Sandy? Sara?"

"Susan," Val supplied. "You don't think she's behind all this, do you?"

"How pissed was she?" Seth asked.

"Somewhere between incredibly and extremely," Val answered with a laugh. Chance seemed uncomfortable with the topic and for some purely mean reason, she found that pretty satisfying.

"That was years ago," Chance insisted. "I'm sure she got over it."

"I think you mean over you," Val corrected.

"Have I missed something?" Seth asked. "Have you figured out who or what is behind Dora's death?"

"Dora and Kent." Val took Seth over to the sofa and filled him in on their discussions.

Seth took some notes, then asked, "No one else has had access to this building?"

"Not that we know of," Chance replied. "Whoever is doing this must have somehow done something to the computer so they could monitor Dora's medical records. They waited for the right opportunity and managed to mix up the prescriptions. Once I get the medical records on Kent Dawson, I can figure out how that order got changed."

Seth appeared skeptical. Val's gut mirrored that thought, but she was so impressed at Chance's proactive posture that she held her tongue.

"I'll run Dora and Kent Dawson through the system and see if anything comes up. Maybe they're linked in some way."

"Thanks." Chance and his brother shared a quick embrace before Seth went on his way.

"Even if you find a link between Kent and Dora, how does the space heater fit in?"

Chance pondered her question. Nothing of substance sprang to mind. "Maybe whoever wanted Dora and Kent dead is annoyed with you because you support me."

"So does Mrs. Halloway, Tara Bishop and all of your brothers. Why single me out?"

"Maybe they don't understand our relationship." *That would make two of us.* Chance was regretting giving into his impulse to kiss Val. All that had been accomplished was to further complicate his life. Something he didn't need right now.

"I'll make up the guest room," he offered.

"Thanks," Val sounded as discomfited as he felt.

He convinced himself that his retreat to his bedroom was to provide her with some privacy. *Who am I kidding?* His brothers were right—he was a cut-and-run kinda guy. For the first time in his life, he didn't know which direction to take.

"You HAVE to wait!" Val told him, irritated to the very limit of her nerves. She was tired from tossing and turning all night. But she was exhausted because of her mishmash of feelings. It seemed as if her brain had intentionally honed in on the fact that Chance was sleeping in the next room. Maybe sucking in all those toxic fumes had scrambled the brain cells necessary for rational thought.

Lord knew her thoughts hadn't been rational. Nope, they had been downright X-rated. One minute, she could close her eyes and see Chance naked. The next, it was an image of the two of them. She wondered when in hell her brain had turned into an all-night porn channel.

And his attitude wasn't helping any.

"I can sweet-talk my way past the records clerk," Chance insisted.

"The records clerk is a man and he bats for your team, so I don't think you'll impress him into letting you copy a file."

"Okay," Chance relented. "If I can't sweet-talk him, maybe I can intimidate him."

Val grabbed her worn leather purse and quelled the inviting idea of knocking Chance senseless with it. "Go down to the café and get me some coffee. I'll meet you there in a little while."

"When?" It was almost a childish whine.

"I have no idea! Just go and wait."

Val went into the hospital via the service door on the side of the building near the Emergency Room. If she could avoid Benton, then everything else should be easy.

She smiled as she passed familiar faces, even waved to one of the lab techs she had known since high school. Luckily, no one questioned her as she slipped into the door marked Private—Records in fading black paint.

The room smelled like bacon. Heavy metal tunes pulsated from a compact disc player on top of a shelf. There was a single desk off to the left and a few lighted cubicles to the right. A closed door led to a second room, where she knew miles and miles of patient charts were neatly arranged in alphabetical order.

Saying a silent *thank-you* to the god who invented identification badges, Val was spared the necessity of trying to remember the guy's name. He was in his early twenties, though persistent acne made him appear younger. A rumpled but clean white dress shirt was hastily tucked into the waistband of his jeans. He sported a tie that looked like a kindergartner's art project—primary colors with no discernable forms. Thanks to a healthy amount of gel, his dark blonde hair was short and spiked on top. Why on earth would he think looking like he just stuck his finger in an electrical outlet was a good fashion statement?

"Hi, Mike," she greeted with her warmest smile.

"Ms. Greene," he returned easily.

The worn toe of his battered tennis shoes kept time with the music. He continued to play another minute of air guitar and then fell into his chair, as if exhausted from performing an entire air set.

"What can I do for you?"

"Patient follow-up," she said, trying to look flustered as she dug a pad out of her bag. "I'm supposed to contact one of Dr. Landry's patients who was in here last week for tests, but his phone's been disconnected. I was hoping the hospital had gotten updated information when he was here."

"Who's the patient?"

She flipped past her grocery list and the list

of item numbers she was tracking in an on-line auction. "Dawson. Kent Dawson."

Mike's casual smile stiffened. "Can't release that one to you."

"Benton?" she asked.

"I'm not supposed to let Dr. Landry have access to anything without clearing through his office first." He reached for the multiple line telephone on his desk. Quickly, Val's hand shot out and prevented him from making the call.

"I'm not Dr. Landry," Val tried.

Mike wasn't buying it for a minute. "Dr. Benton won't see it that way."

"He doesn't have to know. C'mon, Mike, cut me a break here."

The young man hesitated for a minute, then relented. Val could have kissed him.

"I hate this boring job anyway," he said before disappearing into the back room.

Impatient, Val paced in the small area. She tapped her fingers on one of the cubicle desks, hoping no one would come in while Mike was doing her bidding.

"One chart. Patient: Dawson, Kent W." Mike slapped the manila folder down on his desk. He kept two fingers on top of it, guarding it from her greedy grasp. "Has Dr. Landry really gone psycho?"

"Of course not!"

"The whole hospital is buzzing. I heard there's a guy from the state police interviewing people right now."

"Then we don't want him to find me here, do we?"

"He's already been here. He watched as I copied the file first thing. Had me do the Simms file and the Mackey file, too."

"Why Moe Mackey?" she asked.

He shrugged. "He didn't say. Dr. Benton already made copies of the same files."

"Then no one should come asking for this a second time, right?"

Mike relented. "I guess not."

"I should probably get the other two files, as well." The records clerk shrugged and Val thanked him.

He returned a few minutes later with the two additional charts. Val moistened her fingertip and continued to search through Kent Dawson's file for the near-fatal test order. Absently, she thanked Mike again as she struggled with the page stuck to the back of the one she sought.

After finally getting the pages separated, she noticed the smudge on her thumb. She glanced at her thumb, then back to the order. "Is this a copy?"

"Nope. The original," Mike verified. "Why?"

There was a perfect mirror image of Chance's signature on the pad of her thumb. Val licked her forefinger and blotted it against his signature. The same result.

Excited by her discovery, Val shoved the charts into her bag and rushed from the room. It was a struggle to walk at a normal pace. She was sure she had found the first piece of important information.

As soon as she exited the hospital, she began to jog through the parking lot, toward the cross street. She wasn't going to wait for a cab. There was sufficient adrenaline coursing through her veins to get her the two miles into town. She couldn't wait to show Chance what she had found. Val cut through the backyards of three homes, then over a block and toward Jasper Park.

She ran to Mountain Road, more exhilarated than ever. A thin sheen of perspiration cooled her face as she continued. Her pace never faltered. As she ran, her bag felt as if it weighed as much as a small child. The soft leather satchel pounded into her lower back in rhythm with her foot falls. As she neared the street, she turned her upper body sideways in order to negotiate her way through two parked cars and then sprinted toward the park.

She took two strides, then felt herself being flung into the air. There was the sound of a car horn, then maybe a scream.

Then nothing.

Chapter Twelve

Hearing that someone had been hit by a car, Chance raced out of the café and about a hundred yards south to where a crowd had gathered. Without polite civility, he shoved his way through the gawking onlookers.

"She ran into the street!" Tara was crying.

He felt his heart stop when he found Tara kneeling over Val's motionless body.

"Thank heavens!" Tara wailed. "Dr. Landry, she hasn't moved!"

Chance felt for a pulse and his own returned when he found one. Ever so gently, he felt along the base of Val's skull, further relieved when he didn't find an obvious break.

"Did someone call 911?"

"I did," Tara said. "I called on my cell."

Chance straddled Val's body, making sure his weight was on his own knees as he stabilized her neck. His brain registered the sound of approaching sirens. "Everyone get to the curb. Give the ambulance room to get through!"

Relief washed over him for the second time in as many days when Val's beautiful eyes opened. Offering a reassuring smile, he cautioned her, "Stay perfectly still."

Typically, she didn't listen. Her hand started toward her forehead but was trapped by his body. "You're sitting on me."

"You might have a—"

"I ran in front of a car!" Val gasped as she remembered. "I must have scared the driver to death. Is he okay?"

"It was Tara," Chance explained. "And I think she's more upset than you are."

"Tara?" Val called. "Get off, Chance."

"Not a hope in hell, Valerie. The only place you're going is to the hospital. Strapped to a backboard until a dozen radiologists tell me you don't have a fracture."

"I can feel my feet and I—"

"I thought I killed you," Tara cried as she

fell to the ground. "I'm so sorry, Val. I couldn't stop. It all happened so fast!"

"I'm the one who's sorry, Tara. I was distracted by— Oh, Chance, *great* news!"

"Hush! You can tell me your news after you've been checked from head to toe."

"But!"

Any further protests were cut short by the arrival of the paramedics. Though she complained nonstop, she was strapped to a backboard and wheeled into the ambulance.

Chance followed her to the hospital, thanks to Seth's police escort. He was about to go into the curtained area where she was being triaged when he was stopped by a stern nurse. "We're getting her into a gown, Dr. Landry."

Though he didn't want to, he reluctantly went out to the waiting room where Seth was standing off to one side, talking into the radio he had clipped to the shoulder of his uniform.

"I've got to get back to the scene," he told Chance.

"I'm sure she's fine. You can hear her griping all the way down the hall."

"Then how come you look like someone just shot your dog?"

"You didn't see her laid out in the middle of the street." Chance fell into a nearby seat, feeling the effects of all the adrenaline draining from his system. "I've seen her like that twice in twenty-four hours."

"Today looks like an accident," Seth assured him. "A couple of dozen people saw her hauling ass toward the park. Personally, I thought she had more sense than to run into the street."

"That was my fault," he admitted. Purposefully, he lowered his voice, cognizant of his surroundings. "She was rushing to meet me at the café. She had to get the medical records. Benton has pretty much nixed my access around here."

"I could have gotten them, Chance."

He shook his head. "One Landry with his butt in a sling is plenty. Lifting confidential medical records could get you in a world of trouble. Val's already privy to them, so even if we get caught, she can blame it on me and I take the heat as her employer. Besides, you're doing your part."

"I should hear something by this afternoon," Seth assured him. "Call me and let me know she's okay."

"I will," Chance said just as the nurse came and got him.

"She's pretty feisty," the nurse opined. "Won't let any of the doctors touch her. Says its you or she's leaving AMA."

"Val's always been an 'against medical advice' kind of person."

Chance found her staring furiously at the ceiling. Her eyes were as fierce as fireballs and he half expected them to shoot thunderbolts at any moment.

"You called?"

"Wipe that look off your face," she warned. "This backboard is absolutely draconian. Tell them to take it off and give me back my clothes."

"Has she been to X ray?"

"Not yet," the nurse supplied. "They're ready for her."

"I am fine," Val insisted. "I can feel all of my fingers and toes. Everything wiggles just fine, thank you very much."

Chance stepped on the brake release for the bed and pushed her in the direction of the corridor. "If you keep complaining, I won't make this ride fun."

"Look down, Chance. Watch as I make one finger in particular work."

He laughed. "If you make an obscene gesture, I'll note it in your chart."

"Speaking of charts—"

"What are you doing?" Benton's voice bellowed down the corridor.

Chance didn't stop. He continued the few feet until he swung the bed in a wide arc in order to get it into the X-ray room.

"Landry!" Benton yelled again. This time his voice vibrated off the walls in the room.

"She needs X rays, Benton. Go check the board—she was hit by a car."

"I read the board," Benton spit back. "Miss Greene will get the same exceptional care as any other trauma victim brought into this hospital. But she won't get it from you. You're privileges have been suspended."

"Miss Greene feels differently," Chance countered. "She specifically requested that I—"

"I don't care if she had the Surgeon General of the United States assign you as her personal physician. You have one minute before I have security escort you back to the chairs."

Chance was prepared to suggest what Benton could do with a chair when Val spoke up.

"Dr. Landry is my personal physician. He isn't issuing orders. So you have no reason to banish him to the waiting room."

"Miss Greene, you are—"

"A patient here, Dr. Benton. A patient currently strapped to a wooden board awaiting an X ray to rule out spinal fracture and/or skull fracture. If anyone here is jeopardizing my standard of care, it's you."

Benton steamed for a second and then barked, "This man doesn't dispense so much as an aspirin."

"That was fun," the X-ray tech whispered as she jerked the machine over the top of Val's bed. She placed a slate with film into a compartment under Val's head and neck. "Any chance you could be pregnant?"

"Not even a remote one," Val answered.

"It sucks being single in this town, doesn't it?" She sighed, then turned to Chance and said, "Get behind the shield with me, Dr. Landry. I wouldn't want to be responsible for damaging future generations."

"We can't have that," Chance agreed easily.

"Take a breath and hold it."

Val did as instructed. There was a grinding sound, followed by a loud click.

"You can breathe."

The process was repeated half a dozen times. Once her head and neck were cleared by the radiologist, the horrible backboard was removed. For the first time, Val was aware of stinging on her right side. She looked down and realized she had quite the pavement burn on her arm. There was a cut on her hand somewhere, she could tell by the blood streaks on her palm.

Chance took her back to the curtained area and gently took her injured hand in his. "Doesn't look too deep. It should be irrigated."

He looked up and Val saw the frustration in his eyes. He was exactly right, but the nurse standing nearby hadn't moved. She was a human reminder of the fact that his career was on hold, perhaps over.

"Do it back at the office?" Val asked.

He shook his head. "I'm sure one of the attendings will be in after a minute."

"I'm sorry, Dr. Landry, but—"

He raised his hand to silence the nurse. "No need to apologize."

"I'll get Dr. Martine," she said, then disappeared.

"I've been dying to tell you what I discovered," Val began.

"Literally," Chance countered. He was still holding her injured hand. "You took about a dozen years off my life, Valerie."

Her head cocked to one side. "Valerie, huh? I feel like I'm about to be sent to the principal's office."

"You should be punished for doing something so reckless. You could have been killed."

"But I wasn't," she dismissed. "Will you listen?"

Dr. Martine arrived then, looking incredibly uncomfortable trying to treat Val and Chance as if they were regular patients. His manner was stiff and stilted as he explained that Val's X rays were fine.

"I'm going to wash your wound now. I don't think it will require stitches."

She smiled at the first-year physician. "Thanks. Then can I go?"

"You lost consciousness, Val. I hear this is the second time since yesterday. You really should let me admit you. At least for one night."

"That's ridiculous," she argued, looking to Chance for support. "Tell him!"

"I happen to agree with him. In less than twenty-four hours, you've been gassed and run over by a car. A night in the hospital sounds like a good plan."

Dr. Martine relaxed a little, but Val looked fit to be tied. "Traitor."

"C'mon, Val. It's just one night. I'll sleep better knowing you're here."

"I can sleep at home," she persisted.

"You've got a concussion, Val," Chance argued. "Really nice nurses will wake you up every couple of hours."

"I can set an alarm at home."

"Humor me, Val. After all, I am your personal physician. You told Benton that a few minutes ago. You weren't lying, were you?"

She relented, but only with the stipulation that Chance had to deliver her some real food and bring clothing and other necessities once she was admitted.

Community Hospital was small, but it was essentially no different than any other hospital. It took slightly over two hours before Val was assigned a space on the second floor.

The antiseptically white room had starving-artist-sale artwork on two walls. One picture—a beachscape complete with seagulls and driftwood in the foreground—hung askew. After some negotiation, Val was permitted to forgo the traditional drafty hospital gown in favor of surgical scrubs.

Her duty nurse was a single mother named Terri, who was mildly chatty but pleasant. She made certain that Val was clear with the layout of the room.

"If you want anything, just give a ring."

"I'll be fine," Val assured her. "I can watch daytime court shows."

"Don't you love those?" Terri laughed. "I always feel better about myself when I see some of those losers airing their pathetic grievances on television."

Smiling, Val agreed. "It is amazing to discover just how many women put their irresponsible boyfriend's cell phones on their credit cards."

"But usually only after they've caught him cheating with their cousin, their best friend and their ex-girlfriend."

"Sometimes I think we should be called the gullible sex instead of the fairer sex."

Terri adjusted the stethoscope dangling around her neck. "We are our own worst enemies. I married an older man thinking he'd be settled and stable. Ten years into it, he decides to recapture his youth by sleeping with one."

"Ouch." Val shifted to sit cross-legged on top of the crisply made bed.

Terri's smiled widened. "Yeah, well, God punished him. His college coed decided she wanted a family. He's currently sixty-five and about to be a father—again. I like to think of them as Beauty and The Nearly-Deceased."

Val was still laughing when Chance appeared in the doorway. Seeing him framed there—a backpack slung over his shoulder, a single rose clasped in his hand, a brilliant smile on his face—nearly stole her breath.

Terri gave Chance a thorough once-over, and then gave Val a wink and a thumbs-up. "I'd put his cell phone in my name any day. Ring if you need me."

After Terri departed, Chance came in, deposited the backpack on the floor and placed the flower in her bedside water pitcher. "Gonna explain that cell phone comment?"

Val shook her head. "Girl stuff—you wouldn't understand."

"You look better," he commented. Chance dragged the chair next to her bed and sat down. "How's the arm?"

Extending her arm, Val examined the road rash and the bandage just above her wrist. "Nothing major. Probably won't even leave a scar. I think I know what happened to Kent Dawson."

"Really? What did you find?"

Unfortunately, the ink on her fingers had been washed away when her cut was treated in the E.R., but it didn't matter. "All orders sent on the interface are printed with smudge-proof ink on special paper."

"Okay."

She glanced around the room. "I need my purse. The order in Kent's file looked legitimate, but it wasn't. It wasn't your signature. My guess is someone scanned your signature into a computer, then ran the actual order through an ink jet."

"How would someone know to do all that?" Chance asked. "If someone wanted Kent to die, wouldn't it be simpler just to shoot him?"

"Of course. Whoever did this had to know you were Kent's doctor. Familiarize himself with the system we use. Get a copy of your signature. Scan it into a computer. Get a copy of the order out of the scheduling office here. Change the order, affix the bogus signature. Then get it back into the admissions office before the test was scheduled."

"Sounds like it would have been simpler just to shoot him," Chance stated. "That's a hell of a complicated plan."

"I agree," Val said. "It does require a lot of steps. And a lot of opportunities for the plan to fail." She reached for the sealed plastic bag that contained her belongings. "Where is my purse?"

"That big leather thing?" Chance queried. "I don't remember seeing it, but it could have been knocked anywhere when you were hit."

Val noticed the deep lines of concern flanking his mouth. "Don't look so horrified, Chance. No harm done. Except that I need my purse."

He blew a breath outward and upward, then rested his head in his hands. Strain and fatigue clouded his handsome features. "You can get another purse. I'm just glad you weren't hurt."

"Yes, you'd be lost without me to keep your ducks in a row."

"It isn't just that." His expression grew more serious, his gaze held hers. Val felt a strange tension string between them. Stretching taut with each second of awkward silence.

So what the hell is it? she wanted to scream. Fearful that his answer wouldn't be what she wanted to hear, Val was unable to say anything. What could she say? *Gee, Chance, did one kiss convince you that you've been secretly pining for me for years? Did seeing me crumpled in the street suddenly make you realize that you can't live without me? Lord!* Maybe she had suffered brain damage after all.

She couldn't stand the silence any more. "Don't get all profound on me, Chance. Remember, I'm the one who steals from you."

"Everything is complicated now, Val. When I kissed you—"

"Please!" she interrupted, not wanting a full postmortem. "It was no big deal."

One dark brow arched questioningly. "Really?"

"Of course. We've both been a little crazy lately with everything's that's happened. Don't read anything into it. I didn't."

"Really?" he repeated, but she got the distinct impression it was a rhetorical question. "Shouldn't we talk about—"

"Finding my purse?"

"That was a pretty abrupt change of subject."

She felt her shoulders slump. "I'll work on transitional phrases later. We need to stay focused. Find my purse so we can look at Dora and Moe's files."

"Moe?" Chance seemed genuinely surprised.

She nodded. "His death was probably an unfortunate natural occurrence, but I still think we should check."

"I'll call Seth," Chance said, reaching for the bedside phone. "He's probably got your purse."

Val sat impatiently by while Chance telephoned his brother. All she heard were affirmative grunts and single words, but she saw the change in Chance's expression.

When he replaced the receiver, Val fought the urge to shake him until he shared what had so obviously intrigued him.

"What?"

"Seth found a connection between Dora and Kent."

Chapter Thirteen

"It's seven-ten," Chance greeted when he found her showered, dressed and pacing in her hospital room.

"I've been calling you since five," she reminded him. "I can't believe you're so calm! I could hardly sleep last night wondering what Seth has found."

"Yes," he acknowledged with a smile. "I remember you telling me that when you called at midnight, at two, at three and at—"

"Hey, spending the night here was your idea. If I had to get up every few hours for a vitals check, it seemed only fair that you share in a little of that karma."

"Punishment," he corrected. Chance handed her a sweater. "It's only in the mid-fifties and, in case you hadn't noticed, the sun isn't up yet."

Grabbing the sweater, she shoved her arms into the sleeves. "Is Seth in his office?"

"No, he's kissing his wife, or at least he was a few minutes ago."

"You Landrys are a lazy bunch. Must be all that disposable income."

"Jealous," he said against her ear as she began to walk past him.

He had intended it to be nothing more than a friendly taunt—teasing between friends. That was until he caught the floral scent of her freshly shampooed hair. After that, he was back in the tunnel of confusing thoughts that had haunted his subconscious all night long.

It was like standing in the middle of a freezing lake, standing on a precarious chunk of ice. Somewhere deep inside, he knew he would have to pick a direction and jump; he just didn't like the choices. If he stood still, the chunk of ice would sink and he'd drown. If he jumped and missed, he would sink and drown. But if he jumped and hit it just right, he'd be in paradise.

When did I start thinking in metaphors? he

wondered as he followed Val out to the nurse's station. She went back to her room for a second and then emerged carrying the rose he had brought her the previous day.

Chance schooled himself not to read anything into that. After all, it was just a flower. Still, part of him wanted to know that it was important to her. His life was seriously less complicated two weeks ago.

And it wasn't just the tragic events that had him off balance. Things were just easier when he lived within his set limits. Having pleasant relationships with women that didn't include any complications was simple. He knew the game and he knew the rules.

This wasn't a game. This was Val.

No, this was trouble.

"Let's go," she urged, folding the discharge orders and slipping them into the pocket of her jeans,

Jeans, he noticed, that fit like a second skin. He was a half step behind her as they headed to the elevator. That presented an opportunity he should have resisted, but he just couldn't. She walked with confidence, probably oblivious to the fact that her stride was sexy as hell. Unlike the fashion, Val had hips. Real hips—the kind of curves that draw a man's attention. Chance was feeling very manly just then.

Uncomfortably manly.

Still, he didn't seem capable of averting his eyes. She had a tight little tush and legs that seemed to go on for a week. Imagining those legs wrapped around him very nearly caused him to groan out loud. Instead, he held Val's bag in front of him, praying that no one— especially Val—would notice his body's predictable but adolescent reaction.

"You're quiet," Val said as the elevator began its descent.

Thinking with the wrong head didn't seem like an appropriate answer, so he just shrugged.

"I feel naked without a purse."

Her remark didn't help him much. Not when his brain envisioned her naked—with and without a purse.

"Chance!"

His attention snapped back to the present and he found her holding the elevator door open for him.

"Are you getting off?"

Don't go there! he silently warned. "You have no idea," he muttered as he stepped into the lobby.

Thankfully, the combination of crisp morning air and a little physical distance helped get him back on track. After helping Val climb into the passenger seat, he went around and slipped behind the wheel. The sun was just climbing above the ridges east of town as they drove the few miles into Jasper.

Seth's Jeep was parked out front of his office.

They entered through the double doors, then weaved between two desks in order to get to Seth's office. Static from the scanner crackled in the quiet space. Seth stepped out from a back room, holding three mugs of steaming coffee by the handles.

"How are you doing?" his brother asked Val, bending to kiss her cheek before receiving an answer.

"I'm fine," Chance answered for them both, annoyed by Seth's comfort and familiarity. It was a stupid overreaction, one he didn't want to think about. "I'll take those." He gave one cup to Val and kept the other for himself.

Pausing long enough to doctor his coffee to his liking, Chance joined Val and his brother inside the office. The door was left open, mainly because no one else had come in yet.

Seth brushed through the papers on his desk, then pulled out a folder and handed it over.

"This case goes back twelve years," he explained. "I don't remember the trial."

Chance tried hard not to be distracted by Val leaning into him as she read from the file in his hand. Tried but failed. He was only human and, as such, ignoring the fact that her breast was pressed against his forearm was akin to ignoring a nuclear explosion.

He had to reread the same sentence three times before comprehension dawned. "They were on a jury?"

"The Turner trial," Seth supplied.

"I remember that," Val said. "He was the first husband convicted of marital rape in this county."

"I found the old case file." Seth handed

over another folder. "No one who worked the case in this office is still alive."

"What about Turner?" Val asked. "Is he still in prison?"

Seth shook his head. "He served the full twelve and was released three months ago."

Chance felt a rush of excitement. "Do you know where he is?"

Seth shook his head, "Still checking. Unfortunately, his conviction predates the sexual offender registration laws in this state. That, plus the fact that he served his full sentence, allows him to wander free among us."

"Wonderful."

"What about the trial transcript?" Val asked.

"Over at the courthouse. I called late yesterday and asked the Clerk of Court to pull it from the archives. Martha said you could come by anytime after eight."

"Thanks," Chance said with feeling. "Mind if we hang out here for another twenty minutes?"

"Feel free."

"What about Moe Mackey?" Val pressed. "Can you run his name to see if he was connected to this trial?"

"Sure."

"Oh, and can I have my purse?"

Seth returned a blank stare.

"Big, brown, leather and heavy?" she provided. "I had it over my shoulder when I ran into the street. My whole life is in that bag."

"I don't think we have it. Hang on and I'll check. Maybe one of the witnesses picked it up. People do that."

"Great."

Seth patted Val's shoulder as he came around the desk. "Don't worry—they almost always return things they pick up at accident scenes. Usually without the money."

Seth stepped out to run Mackey's name through the law enforcement computer system.

"That stinks," Val groaned. "I've got the three files we need in my bag."

"I'm sure it will show up. If not, we can just make another copy."

"No we can't," Val told him. "I took the originals. Mike in the records office and I figured it was better if they disappeared altogether than if someone found me there making copies."

Chance breathed heavily. "That wasn't a great plan."

"I was winging it," she retorted.

"I knew I should have gone with you."

"Hindsight is always crystal clear."

Seth came back holding a large envelope. He opened it and retrieved a stack of photographs.

Chance refilled his coffee and then returned to find Seth still thumbing through the pictures. "I don't see a purse anywhere."

Val picked up the pictures and glanced through them herself. "Me, either. So now what?"

"Cancel your credit cards. Call your bank."

"Cell phone provider, yeah, yeah. Any chance you could contact the witnesses?"

"I'll touch base with them, sure," Seth agreed. "You might want to check with the paramedics, too. Sometimes a purse gets shoved into the ambulance and gets lost in the confusion."

"Thanks," Val said, offering him her best smile. "And thanks for yesterday."

"It was all over by the time I got there," Seth commented. "By the way, I do need to get your statement some time soon. Tara's insurance company will probably need it to keep her insurance rates from skyrocketing."

"It wasn't her fault," Val insisted, feeling a renewed wave of guilt.

"I know. Everyone said you ran between the truck and the car parked along Mountain."

"I did. Totally my stupidity."

"Just be glad no one was hurt."

That was certainly the up side to the incident. Val made a mental note to send Tara a card apologizing for the incident. Maybe even a basket of teas or something.

A few minutes later, she was walking beside Chance on the way to the courthouse. "Do you think Tara would like biscuits or muffins better?"

"What?"

"I'm thinking of sending Tara a little gift basket. Should I send muffins or biscuits?"

"How would I know? I've only spoken a couple of dozen words to the girl in my life. But, if you want my opinion, I'd send muffins."

"Why?"

"They taste better."

"You don't even know what they taste like. I haven't told you where I'm ordering from."

"Doesn't matter," Chance said, placing his hand at the small of her back. "Biscuits are always dry and boring."

"Not always," Val argued. Not that she had any strong affinity for biscuits. She was just trying to keep her mind focused on something other than the feel of his fingers splayed along her spine.

Everything seemed strained all of a sudden. Well, it wasn't totally sudden. Ever since she had kissed his socks off, Chance had been strange. The reaction that had pleased her immensely had backfired. She had hoped that treating the situation in an adult, casual fashion might prevent things from getting weird. But what choice did she have? That was the only reaction she knew he would understand. She had spoken and acted in a fashion she felt he would appreciate. She had tried—and apparently failed—to treat the moment with mature perspective.

Maturity was something seriously missing from her current state of mind. There was something decidedly girlish about her fascination. They were walking a few hundred feet. A simple, uncomplicated thing that shouldn't have required thought. Yet this time, on this walk, her brain was overloaded with thoughts. Most of them carnal or unrealistic.

The carnal ones were easier to handle than the unrealistic ones. Being a normal, healthy woman over the age of consent, it was perfectly understandable that she should be intrigued by the feel of his fingertips hovering above the waistband of her jeans. She should have a female awareness of the fact that his hip brushed her body with alternating strides. She had just as many hormones as the next woman. Those were the easy things.

The rough part came when she allowed her thoughts to drift down the closed passage of possibilities. With Chance, there were no possibilities. Only reality. Anything more than friendship was bound to end with a broken heart. Hers. Chance didn't do happily-ever-after and she wasn't going to settle.

Why? her brain challenged. Theoretically, it didn't have to be all or nothing. She was fairly sure that Chance could be coaxed into an affair. It would be great while it lasted. Then what? "You can never go back."

"Go where?" he asked.

Val stared at the steps, not realizing she had spoken aloud. "I—I want my purse back."

Chance's laughter teased her ears. "Why are women so attached to their handbags?"

"It's the female equivalent of a remote control."

They met the helpful clerk, who directed them into a small room and left them alone with three volumes of bound pages. "Who knew a two-day trial was so wordy?" Val complained as she opened one of the books.

"Lawyers tend to use twenty words when five will do the trick."

"And doctors don't," she teased.

"No, we don't. Doctors must be precise."

"Precise?" she grinned across the scarred table at him. "Is that what you call saying *laceration* instead of *scratch* or *foreign body* instead of *splinter*?"

"It just assures patients that we learned something during all those years of schooling."

"Personally, I always thought it was more important to know how to use a scalpel than a thesaurus."

"You hold the profession in such low esteem. Why did you go into medicine in the first place?"

"I liked the mystery of medicine."

"Kind of like being a detective, huh?"

"Yes, but then I saw how most of the emphasis was on the ailment or the disease instead of the person."

"Not all doctors are uncaring jerks, Val."

"I know that," she insisted. "I just realized that I wouldn't fit, so I took a different path."

"But you were so close."

"And I thought about sticking it out," she admitted. "But I was carrying student loans up to my eyeballs and the debt compounded almost daily and I wasn't going to gain anything by continuing. It made personal and financial sense for me to leave school and work alongside a doctor instead of becoming one."

Chance was contemplatively silent for a moment. Then he said, "That makes sense."

It shouldn't have mattered that Chance understood and respected her choice. But it did. Val felt like the kid in first grade picked to be line leader.

"You bring an important perspective," Chance continued. "It's good—within reason—for people to explore alternative cures and treatments."

"Thanks, I think. That was a backhanded compliment if ever there was one."

"I only meant that there's alternative options and then there's suicide."

"I have never advocated a cancer patient running into the jungle and sucking on berries instead of an appropriate, recommended course of chemo."

"You're right and I wasn't insinuating you did." Chance took the other binder. "I actually agree with your stance on a cautious use of antibiotics and those food guidelines you put together for my diabetic patients."

"Don't forget the recipes. I spent many hours in my kitchen testing those recipes."

"You are an invaluable asset. Every doctor should have a PA like you."

"Yes, they should. Let's read. All that talk about my culinary skills has reminded me that I've missed a few meals."

"We can go to the café first, if you'd like."

"Nope, work first, food second."

"That's one of the many differences between men and women." His stomach growled as if to punctuate his observation.

Val found most of the transcript boring and drawn out. Carl Turner and his wife had been separated for five years at the time he broke into her home, raped her and beat her. It was only because of a disjointed 911 call made by her youngest son that an ambulance was called to her aid. The second grader had awakened and found his mother bleeding and unconscious. Val cringed at the thought of what that scene must have done to such a young child. The poor kid was probably scarred for life.

Turner was identified, arrested, jailed and tried. It was only while Turner was in jail awaiting trial that his wife found an attorney willing to handle her divorce pro bono. She got to take the stand to vividly and tearfully recount the horror of the attack.

Val's appetite was a thing of the past by the time she finished reading the testimony. Even twelve years later, it was emotionally draining.

"What a vile man," she said, shoving the folder away and rubbing her tired eyes. "He should have gotten life."

Chance seemed equally disturbed. "Life chained to a wall by his—"

"That, too. Turner never claimed he didn't rape his wife. Only that the sex was consensual."

"I got that, too," Chance admitted. "So it doesn't seem logical that he would harbor a grudge against members of his jury for twelve years."

"I know. I didn't get the sense that Turner has the smarts to pull this off, either."

"It's hard to imagine a guy who dropped out of the third grade arranging a complicated scheme that requires at least a passing understanding of medical terms and procedures."

"And some computer savvy," she reminded him.

Defeat pretty much dripped from his features. "So the jury connection is a bust. That leaves only one other explanation."

"What?"

"Me," Chance answered.

Chapter Fourteen

"You have some reason for wanting Dora and Kent dead?" Val asked.

Chance shook his head as he led Val out of the courthouse. "I'll explain while we eat."

"Let's go to your place."

He forced a smile. "Propositioning me?"

"Hardly. I'm not hungry but I'll make you something. You can eat while I make some calls. I have copies of my account information for my credit cards and things in my desk at the office."

Thoughts ricocheted back and forth in his brain as they drove to his place. Nothing seemed to want to gel. It was as if the answer were there—just out of his grasp.

Kind of like his feelings for Val. Just a few feet away, she was busy in his kitchen, preparing some sort of elaborate omelet. The table was set for one and fresh coffee dripped into the carafe. The scene was as comforting as it was disturbing.

Comforting in that it simply seemed right. He never let female friends cook for him. There was something too familiar, too intimate about that. It implied things he normally didn't want misconstrued. There were certain things that meant couple and commitment, two words he had tried to ban from his everyday life. You didn't let a woman keep things at your place or vice versa. No pink razors or moisturizer were allowed in his bathroom. He had never cleared out a dresser drawer or a shelf in the medicine cabinet. Never wanted to. Until now.

Which brought him squarely into the realm of disturbing. It was scary enough that he was lusting for Val. There was a real potential for screwing up an important friendship if he explored those feelings. But the other things he was imagining were terrifying. He could easily remember the crushing tightness in his chest when he'd found her on the sofa. The ease with which those intense feelings returned when he caught sight of her lifeless body in the middle of the street. Val was important to him on many levels. He was fine with acknowledging how vital she was to his practice. How very much he respected her knowledge and skills. She was a devoted and trusted friend. Chance had known for years that Val would always tell him the truth. She was quick to give him advice even when he didn't really want her counsel. Usually, she was right on target, even when it took him a few days and a bout of temper to reach that conclusion.

Those were friend levels. They were safe. In the last few days, he had seen glimpses of another level—another place. And it scared him to death.

Nothing about Val would be easy or uncomplicated, his two favorite adjectives for relationships. He could never give her what she expected. The alternative was to give her what he could—and hope she could accept that as enough.

"Come and eat," she called. Val placed a huge plate of food on the table. "You need to shop, Chance. You remember that food pyramid pasted all over the office? It has pictures of apples and other things called fruits and vegetables."

"Good tip," he shot back with a grin before diving into the omelet. "Assuming I don't have to save your life today, I'll make a note to drop by the grocery."

"Are you going to hold that over my head forever?"

"Probably!" he called as she raced downstairs to the office.

Val was grateful for the distance, such that it was. She sincerely hoped that a little space would enable her to get a grip on herself. Or more accurately, on her raging libido.

She felt his eyes follow her every move as she made him eggs. The experience made her strangely aware of everything. The last time she had worried about how her hair looked from the back she was fifteen and madly, passionately in love with Harold Listman. What was next? Getting relationship advice from a psychic?

Sex is next, her brain answered. Clearly, calmly and directly. Even though it wasn't something she wanted to admit, it was true.

Grabbing the phone, she used a pencil

eraser to punch in the customer service number for her bank. She was immediately tangled in the web of an automated voice messaging system. "When did human beings stop answering telephones?" she groused, pressing seven for the third time. "I'm glad my call is important to you," she challenged the recorded voice. "I'll wait right here for the next available representative to take my call in the order in which it was received."

Instead of music, she was looped into a series of commercials advertising all of the bank's services. "Screw direct deposit. I'd rather have a direct line to a breathing person."

As the wait continued, Val activated the speaker feature on the phone, and then powered up the computer to access patient records. If Chance was the link between Dora, Kent and Moe, maybe there was something about their records that would suggest a direction.

Nothing jumped out. She had to stop for a minute when a live voice came over the speaker. After explaining what had happened, giving her account number, the last four digits of her Social Security number, answering the security question and providing a password, she was able to safeguard her checking account, her ATM card and her credit card.

She spent another half hour repeating the process with her cell phone company and the department store card she carried. All that was left was to replace her driver's license.

By the time she was finished, she knew every illness, operation, test, and symptom ever suffered by Dora, Kent and Moe. If there was some sort of connection, she didn't see it. Nothing overlapped, nothing matched. Different birthdays, no patterns in their appointments, nothing. It was as frustrating as her sex life.

Val rolled her eyes. She was wondering when her mind would stop bringing every topic around to her carnal longings.

Trying a new tactic, she typed in a second order for the same GI test listing all the same information as was on the original but using herself as the patient.

She had to go into the other room to retrieve the hard copy. The page barely had time to exit the machine when she grabbed it. Unfortunately, her little test failed. The order was perfect—right test, right name, everything.

"Damn," she muttered as she crumpled it up and put it in the trash can.

"Problem?" Chance asked.

He smelled of woodsy cologne and masculinity. An annoying lump lodged in her throat. His easy smile reached his dark eyes. He was just gorgeous.

As if reading her thoughts, Chance wordlessly moved forward, catching her around the waist and pulling her against him. Then he hesitated.

Val knew she had only to say one word and this wouldn't happen. This was her last chance. It remained unspoken, but she knew the reason for his hesitation. The terms were his, but the decision was hers. He was offering nothing more than that.

Reaching her hand up into his dark hair, she pulled his mouth to hers. Need overwhelmed reason. Since the alternative was nothing, she would readily take Chance on any terms.

Chance was relieved and pleased when Val's lips touched his. The scent of her perfume had vanquished most of his ability to reason. He should feel guilty, knowing he was the wrong person for her and still wanting this to happen. Somewhere between the feel of her fingers laced in his hair and the urgent tilt of her body, wanting had given way to a real, palpable need.

They could sort out their differences on commitment later. He just wanted to concentrate on the surges of pleasure coming at him from every direction.

He lifted his head, studying each of her features in turn. Drawing power and courage from the desire he saw in her eyes.

His fingers moved to her throat, gently testing her pulse point. Erratic little breaths washed over his face and he felt the uneven beat of her heart. Golden starbursts around her pupils seemed to explode with passion. Moving his fingertips under her chin, he lifted her face fractionally. When her tongue flicked out to moisten her lower lip, Chance wasn't sure he could maintain his composure.

Her mouth looked soft, pliant and inviting. Her skin was warm and flushed. Chance allowed his fingertip to trace the line of her jaw. Their eyes locked as his finger dipped lower. It grazed the edge of her blouse. She let out a little half breath that only heightened his arousal. His finger trailed lower, moving aside the fabric until he felt the soft, lacy trim on her bra.

She shifted up onto her toes, trying to reach his mouth. Chance purposefully countered, moving his head away. There was something intoxicating about looking into her eyes as he touched her. He could see tangible signs of his effect on her. Which seemed only fair since his own body's response was pressed against her belly.

"Wait." In spite of speaking a single word, Chance barely recognized the sound of his own voice. Fearing he would give in to his body's demand for fast and immediate gratification, he lifted Val in his arms and carried her into the exam room.

After laying her on the table, he half lay, half leaned next to her. There just wasn't room on the exam table. That realization took a little of the mood out of the moment. A few seconds later, he realized that their every movement caused the paper covering to tear or crinkle. And the sun was beaming in through the window, nearly blinding him.

Chance cursed and shifted. Instead of making things better, they continued to go downhill.

Apparently, his ankle had caught the electrical cord running to the EKG machine. In his fervent desire to free himself, he had yanked the cord. However, the cord had not come free from the wall; rather, the energy traveled in reverse. Several thousands of dollars worth of sensitive medical equipment went crashing to the floor.

"Hold on," Val insisted, rising and leaping off the table.

"This is working out well," he muttered as he peered over to survey the damage.

"It's probably for the best," Val responded.

"Depends on your perspective," Chance countered. His perspective made his jeans a little uncomfortable in the groin area.

The machine was in pieces. Val bent down and began winding the roll of EKG paper that had unraveled across the floor. The top plate had shattered and the ink needle was bent up at attention like an abandoned flag of surrender.

"This is terrible," she said. Then her attention was drawn to an odd mass of gears and electrical tape. "Look at this, Chance!"

He thought about telling her to hell with the machine, let's go upstairs, but there was something urgent in her voice that sounded odd.

"What is that?" He bent down next to her, pushing away plastic shards in order to get an unobstructed view.

Someone had removed the lever that normally held the ink needle. An EKG measured the electrical activity of the heart. The needle had to be supported enough to be suspended over the paper to draw the graph of the heart's activity. But it had to move freely and someone had taped a crudely made set of gears against the needle.

"Turn it on," Chance instructed. He managed to right the broken case and balance the machine on the floor enough to get it to operate. With no patient and no electrodes and no patient, the needle should have simply registered a straight line and an alarm should have sounded.

Instead, there was no alarm and the gears hit the needle so that a precise pattern appeared on the test strip.

"It looks like a normal EKG," Val observed.

"Like Moe Mackey's EKG." Chance felt his gut twist. "First Dora, then Moe."

"Chance!"

Chance rushed to the front desk area when he heard Val call his name.

Val was by the printer holding a piece of paper. She looked up at him, her face a mask of confused concern.

"It gets worse."

Chapter Fifteen

"You want me to order a contrast angiogram?" Chance asked after scanning the page.

"This doesn't make sense," Val told him.

"Not unless you're having heart problems. You're not, are you?"

Touched by his concern, Val tossed him a reassuring grin before going back to the main computer terminal. "There is a serious glitch in the system."

"A computer didn't rig the EKG machine," Chance remarked as he leaned against the desk while she typed furiously. "We need Seth over here. Someone must have broken in."

"Go ahead and call him. This may take a minute or two."

Trying to repeat her previous steps exactly,

she repeated her earlier actions and waited for the printer to spew out the order.

Chance paced impatiently as she read the results. "This is correct," she stated. Five minutes later, just as Seth was coming through the door, she was still waiting for the second order. Nothing.

"I don't get it," Val mused, rechecking the information she had typed into the system.

"Then we are in serious trouble because I am totally confused."

"What's up?" Seth asked.

While Val worked on the computer, Chance revealed what they had discovered inside the EKG machine.

After listening, Seth called for the mobile crime scene unit of the state police. "Have you checked for signs of a break-in?"

"I forgot the allergies!" Val cried out.

"You're allergic to something?" Chance asked.

Tapping the screen, she indicated the entry field that took such conditions into consideration. After entering the same allergies that plagued Kent Dawson, she again sent the order through the system for processing.

"I'm going to have a look around," Seth stated, removing the Maglite from his utility belt.

"You're ordering all these fake tests to prove what?" Chance asked after Seth slipped out the side door.

"Okay," she paused long enough to gather all the pages and her thoughts. "All I did was put in the same information you did before Kent Dawson's hospital mishap. The computer spit out the correct order."

"Proving I didn't make a mistake." Chance's features relaxed slightly.

"A few minutes later, a second order was printed."

"A duplicate?"

"No. The second order was for a test that the computer already knows would have resulted in a potentially fatal reaction.

"So now," she stopped again, retrieving the second sheet of paper as it came out of the machine. "You get this." She passed him the paper. "Which explains part of why Kent Dawson was almost killed."

"So, it had to be someone with access to the office?"

"Not necessarily," Val admitted. "Anyone with enough skill to add a Trojan horse in medical software has probably got enough talent to create a bogus copy and get it over to the admissions office at the hospital."

"But he still needed access to my signature, right?"

She shrugged. "Technology has made it pretty easy to scan, cut, paste and copy. With the right equipment, someone could easily pull your signature off anything from your driver's license to a Christmas card."

"Is there any way to tell if this Trojan horse—by the way, why is it called that?"

"Because of the way it works. Remember Homer's *Iliad*?"

"I knew I should have paid more attention to the travails of the ancient Greeks."

"The Greeks give a giant wooden horse to their foes, the Trojans, ostensibly as a peace offering. But after the Trojans drag the horse inside their city walls, Greek soldiers sneak out of the horse's hollow belly and open the city gates, allowing their compatriots to pour in and capture Troy."

"And this is relevant to a computer how?"

"Someone uploads a harmless-looking file, but hidden inside is a virus that makes the computer system do something it wasn't intended to do."

"Can you just go into your local computer store and buy one of these?"

Val laughed. "No. The person would have to know the targeted program's parameters."

"Is there some way to dissect the computer to find out who did this?"

"I'm sure there is, but we've reached the limit of my computer expertise. Maybe Seth can call a forensic computer person."

"There's such a thing as a computer forensic expert?"

"Who do you think investigates accidents on the information superhighway?"

"Computers suck."

Seth returned with little new information. Chance let Val explain the connection between the Greeks and Kent Dawson's anaphylactic shock.

When she finished, Seth made another call to the state crime lab.

Absorbing all this techno information

made his brain hurt. Seth seemed to be glazing over, as well.

"I'm more comfortable when the criminals have guns and knives," Seth sighed.

"Assuming the techies can sort out all this stuff, we should know who is behind this pretty quick," Chance said.

"I hope so, but I doubt it," Val interjected.

Chance read the hesitation in her eyes as Seth asked, "Why?"

"I don't think this is some high school hacker run amok. It will probably take a lot of time and tedious work for the experts to track this."

"She's right," Seth agreed. "The FBI has had hundreds of agents working on computer crimes and they barely scratch the surface. The nerd squad can work on the technical aspects. Until then, I think it is probably best for you to lie low."

"I've already closed the office." Chance quelled his strong urge to pick up the machine and hurl it out into the street. "It would help if I knew why someone would go to all this trouble."

"Nineteen forty-four. George Cukor film?" Val gushed.

"You've gone from the ancient Greeks to movie trivia?"

She cast Chance a withering glare. "Do you want to mock me or hear my theory?"

"Mock you," he countered. "Just kidding. Go ahead."

"*Gaslight.* Ingrid Bergman married Charles Boyer, who is really a jewel thief who murdered her aunt. He then spends the whole movie making Ingrid Bergman's character think she's losing her grip."

"That's one of Savannah's favorite flicks," Seth interjected.

"Great movie," Val agreed.

"Bergman was very hot in that," Seth agreed with enthusiasm. "She deserved the Academy Award."

"Did you know that was Angela Lansbury's first film?"

"Hey, Roeper and Ebert!" Chance interrupted. "Can we stay focused?"

"Sure," Val said with a smile. "We know the computer was reprogrammed."

Chance picked up the thread. "To make it look as if I suddenly went off the deep end killing my patients."

"Right," Seth agreed. "So who hates you that much?"

"No one," Chance responded instantly.

"Someone does," Val agreed. "Someone who tampered with the EKG machine."

"I don't suppose either of you noticed anyone near the machine?" Seth asked.

Chance didn't recall anything out of the ordinary. "I couldn't even tell you the last time we used it before Moe Mackey. And it isn't like it was kept secured, either."

"The same for the portable heater?"

Chance looked at Val, and then nodded. "Could the same person have tampered with the heater that almost killed Val?"

He watched as the reality of his question hit her. Feeling incredibly impotent, Chance could think of nothing more than to reach out and pull her against him. After giving her a reassuring hug, he turned his attention back to Seth.

"I suppose if someone could rig your EKG machine, they could rig a space heater. Any thoughts?"

"Not a clue," Val admitted. "No one hates *me* that much."

A white van pulled up out front and Seth went out to meet with the team of crime scene investigators who emerged carrying large tackle boxes.

"If someone is trying to destroy you and/or your career, why would they come after me?" Val asked.

He felt her hand slide across his chest as she folded herself into his embrace. "Because you've been supportive of me. Or maybe they think we're together."

"No one who knows you would ever think that."

That should have been a breakthrough observation. It should have made him feel one small step closer to discovering who had killed two of his patients. Instead, it simply reminded him of the huge albatross hanging around his neck. Still, her safety was more pressing than the internal conflict gnawing at the lining of his stomach.

"You need to get out of here. Go someplace safe."

Instead of pulling away from him, she nuzzled closer. "I am safe, Chance."

Annoyed, he gently placed his hands on

her shoulders and moved her to arm's length. Slipping his finger beneath her chin, he forced her eyes to meet his. He didn't see fear so much as he read a steely determination. "No. You aren't. I'm going to put you on a plane to someplace where no one can get to you until I can find out who is doing this. I've already got two deaths on my conscience. I don't want to add a third."

Val's expression didn't falter. In fact, his proclamation seemed to only heighten her resolve. "I wouldn't leave even if I could."

Annoyance bubbled up inside him, settling as a lump in his chest. "There's nothing holding you here."

"Just my life," she tossed back, shrugging out of his reach. "You may like an uncomplicated, unconnected existence, but I don't. And I won't."

"If you're referring to the clinic on the reservation, I can take care of it."

"Sure you can, so long as your vengeful stalker doesn't decide to use you to kill another innocent person."

Fury gripped him. It was a kind of anger he had never before experienced. Val was absolutely correct, but knowing that only added to his sense of utter uselessness. He didn't like being a puppet, especially not when the person pulling his strings was deadly *and* anonymous.

Seth walked into the heated tension that separated them. He seemed to sense as much, and looked from Chance to Val but received no explanation.

"Here's the deal," he began. "I need to print the two of you and anyone else whose fingerprints should be here so they can be excluded."

"Fine."

"Fine," Val echoed.

"Fine, then," Seth agreed. "Who is going first?"

"She is," Chance answered. "Then put her in a cell and keep her there until you have someone in custody."

"Put him in a cage," Val countered. "He's the target, not me."

"Wrong. This lunatic already tried to kill you once. He'll probably try again."

"Time out," Seth said, holding up his hands. "I know you're both a little tense right now, but stop putting the cart before the horse."

Chance gave his brother a questioning look.

Seth sighed. "All we have right now is conjecture."

"How can you say that?" Chance thundered.

"Because right now the only person who had access to the EKG machine, the pharmacy override code, knowledge of Kent's fatal allergy to iodine and the SUV seen leaving Val's house is you," he told Chance.

"I didn't do any of that stuff."

"Chance may be a jerk, but he wouldn't hurt me or anyone else."

"Thanks, I think."

Again Seth played peacemaker. "I know that but I still need to prove it."

"I'm not going to sit on my hands," Chance warned.

"So give me a lead," Seth suggested. "I'm ready and willing to move heaven and earth for you, Chance."

"He's right," Val commented. "We have to stop, take a breath and approach this logically."

Pulling his key out of his pocket, Chance said, "I might know where to start."

Chapter Sixteen

"This is a seriously bad idea."

"You don't have to come. In fact, I would prefer you didn't."

Val ignored him and got into the passenger seat a second before he gunned the engine and squealed out of the parking space.

"You're already in enough trouble with Benton. Harassing his wife isn't going to win you any brownie points."

"Tough," Chance answered.

She watched as they drove west, toward the small but exclusive subdivision where many of Jasper's upwardly mobile professionals lived in large, brick homes with sloping, manicured lawns.

Each home sat on an acre or more of land. While the designs were different, the houses all had a sameness to them. They were tangible steps near the top of the ladder of success. Val had been to Susan Benton's home a couple of times for social gatherings.

"It's the two-story facing the street," she directed, pointing to the home.

A recent-model minivan stood guard over a long driveway rimmed by flowers struggling to take hold of the fickle Montana spring. Parked alongside of the minivan was an adorable little motorized car that had been decorated unevenly with stickers.

A state-of-the-art stroller was near the front door. Val reminded Chance that it wasn't too late to rethink this nutty idea.

He pressed the bell and they waited. "Susan is a nurse, so she'd have the knowledge to have circumvented my medical orders. *And* she hates me."

If Val had misgivings about their visit, it paled in comparison to the reserved greeting they received from Susan.

Even clad in baby-food-stained sweats with her red hair piled in a disorganized mess at the back of her head, she was stunning. And tall.

Val had forgotten that Susan was close to six feet without shoes, which she wasn't wearing. However her toes were perfectly polished in a muted peach that looked like they belonged in some sandal ad.

"Chance?" she said, kind of frozen in the doorway. "Val," she acknowledged with a nervous smile. "I'm afraid my husband is at the hospital."

"I need to see you," Chance told her, stepping inside the foyer quickly.

Val mused that he was probably afraid she might slam the door in their faces. And she wouldn't have blamed the woman in the least.

Her home was cluttered. Toddler and baby items seemed to have invaded every possible inch of the first floor. Underneath it all, Val knew the decor was carefully selected and beautifully appointed. Every room had an individual color scheme, yet it all blended together like a well-designed floral arrangement.

Susan lifted her squirming baby boy out of a swing and called to her young daughter to turn down the cartoon blasting on the television.

It was suburbia at its best.

Susan quieted the baby by resting him on her hip and swaying while she curled his fingers around his thumb. "This is Colton," she introduced, maternal pride in her voice. Turning to Val she added, "You remember Chelsea?" glancing toward her daughter.

"He's beautiful," Val offered, tweaking the baby's cheek. "Six months late, but congratulations."

"Thanks," Susan said, visibly relaxing. "What can I do for you?"

"I'm sure your husband has told you what's been happening?" Chance said without preamble.

Val poked her finger into his ribs, not bothering to even invent a pretext. "Chance is on the verge of a complete meltdown," she offered by way of apology for his rudeness.

"I can imagine," Susan replied. "Can I get either of you anything? Coffee? Tea?"

"We didn't come to socialize," Chance began.

"Tea would be great!" Val inserted.

Still swaying with the baby, Susan managed to make tea and put a videotape in for her daughter before moving to the kitchen table. Shoving several crayons and a coloring book off to one side, she cleared a place for them and indicated seats. "Sorry about the mess. I usually wait until the end of the day and then start tossing things in the toy box."

"Susan," Chance started again, "I need to ask you about what's been happening."

Shifting the baby to her shoulder, Susan asked, "Why?"

"We think—"

"No 'we' here," Val corrected.

He shot her a deadly little glance. "I think my patients were harmed by someone wanting to get back at me."

"And you think I...?" Susan laughed, then had the presence to regroup when she realized he was serious. "Oh, Chance. You must be pretty desperate if you've come to me. Why on earth would I need to get back at you?"

Val sat back and enjoyed watching Chance's discomfort. Ego always falls hard.

"You're a nurse and, well," Chance paused, "we, um, ended—"

"Years ago," Susan finished. "I understand that you are under a great deal of pressure,

Chance. Aside from the fact that I am not an evil psychopath, do you really think I've been pretending to be a happily married mother of two just lying in wait to punish you for breaking up with me?"

"Apparently not," Chance admitted. It was obvious that he realized how far-fetched that was. "But your husband is—"

"Jealous," Susan finished. She patted the baby's back. "He has no reason to be. I never thought I could be this happy."

Val looked around and had to agree. Susan had a nice home, cute kids and the luxury of staying home with them. There wasn't even a tiny hint that she was some sort of spurned and scarred ex-lover.

"I'm glad for you," she heard Chance say. She knew him well enough to realize he was sincere. "Your husband is pretty determined to throw me to the wolves."

"He's just insecure, Chance. He's not a spiteful man. He just sees things in black and white. I actually like that about him—no indecision, no half measures. He'll come around and, assuming you aren't nuts, he'll be the first to apologize."

"I doubt that," Chance muttered.

"Cut him some slack, Chance. He went all through medical school in your shadow."

Val sipped her tea as she listened.

"He ends up marrying one of your castoffs."

"I don't think of you like that," Chance insisted.

"I don't really care," Susan retorted with blunt honesty. "The only thing that matters is that *I* don't see myself as a Chance Landry reject. Sure, I did for a couple of weeks after you dumped me, but I got over it. My husband grew up modestly. You had the successful family and the social clout. He thinks you're smarter than he is."

Val kicked Chance under the table, fearful that he might announce an agreement with that observation.

"You're not, by the way," Susan commented with a genuine smile. "He was smart enough to marry me."

"And make beautiful babies," Val added, getting to her feet and tugging Chance along with her. Susan was a very nice woman with a very nice life, but Val wasn't really interested in sitting there to hear a blow-by-blow account of their past relationship.

"That was pretty awkward, don't you think?" she asked when they were safely inside of his car.

"I should have listened to you," Chance admitted easily. "I'm convinced that Susan hasn't thought about me over the years, any more than I have thought of her."

For some reason Val found that comforting. More comforting than she cared to admit. "She got the fairy tale, Chance. Of course she's happy."

He paused and held her gaze. "You sound envious."

She wasn't sure how to react to that. Maybe she was. What was so wrong with wanting a husband and family to round out her life?

I'm in love with a man who doesn't want to marry.

The thought hit her like a sucker punch. Squeezing her eyes shut, she demanded that her subconscious take it back. Pretend the idea never even entered her mind.

Too late.

"Val?"

"Y-yes?"

"I asked, what now?"

Shoot me now? "I want to go home."

"YOU'RE QUIET," Chance observed a little while later when they were standing in her living room. He could have added jumpy and distracted, but he didn't have a handle on her mood and that was disconcerting.

"You don't seem yourself," he said as he began walking in her direction.

A strange calm seemed to come over her, as if she had settled some weighty issue and was comfortable with the outcome. Her pretty face relaxed; there was a sensual serenity about her that his man radar didn't miss. He hated himself for even thinking in that direction. There was too much about his life that was unsettled just now.

He took an involuntary step backward when she was close. The action didn't go unnoticed, not if her satisfied smile was any indication.

"Val," he cautioned as he held one hand, palm out. "Whatever you're thinking, *now* is not the right time. We can't do this."

"I haven't done anything," she purred.

Chance backed up farther, only to find himself against the cool wall. Val kept coming, her intense eyes belying the small smile curving her delicate mouth.

"Please?"

Without a word, Chance took the water bottle from her hand and deposited it on the nearest table. He switched their positions and flattened his palms on the wall on either side of her head. "I'm a human being, Val. You've been virtually mute for a while and suddenly you're like *this*. Stop playing around."

She could smell his musky cologne and hear his slightly uneven breath. There was a smoldering intensity in his dark eyes that sent a ripple of desire into the pit of her stomach.

"Who said I was playing?"

"I have the distinct feeling that I won't respect myself in the morning," he whispered.

His warm, mint-scented breath washed over her face. Tilting her head back, she searched his eyes beneath the thick outline of his eyelashes.

"I know this is the wrong time for this," he said. Then, bending at the waist, Chance leaned forward until his lips barely grazed hers. Wide-eyed, Val experienced the first tentative seconds of the kiss through a haze. The pressure from his mouth increased almost instantly. It was no longer tentative or regretful. It was demanding and confident.

His hands moved slowly, purposefully to her waist. His strong fingers slipped beneath the fabric of her shirt and came to rest just below the swell of her rib cage. Her mouth burned where he incited fires with his expert exploration of her mouth. A sigh inspired by purely animal desire rose in her throat. She was being bombarded with so many sensations at once, one more pleasurable than the last. The warm pad of his thumb brushed the bared flesh at her midriff. His kiss was so thorough, so wonderful that her knees were actually beginning to tremble.

When he pulled away, Val very nearly reached out to keep him close to her. It wasn't necessary; he didn't go far. Resting his forehead on hers, she listened to the harmony of their labored breathing.

"What are we doing?" he rasped.

"I believe you just kissed me."

"I kissed you. You responded. This isn't new. You've always said you couldn't handle my aversion to commitment. Why the sudden change of heart?"

"I've changed my mind," she said, feeling sad and lonely all of a sudden. "So what if we both know this isn't such a great idea?"

"That," he began as he lifted his head and met her eyes, "is one hell of an understatement. In spite of the fact that my conscience will bother me for the rest of my days, I can't help myself, Val. I've wanted you too long to be honorable when you're acting like this."

Chance wasn't subtle with his second kiss. There was nothing even remotely sweet about it. This kiss was meant to do one thing: convey desire. Even before he pressed his hardness into her belly, Val knew he was deeply aroused.

"Wait," she said, a little frightened by the level and suddenness of his passion. Her courage waned a bit under the weight of his honesty. He was telling her nothing new, yet it still pricked a pang of disappointment. Knowing she loved him was now an uncomfortable reality. Convincing herself that she would rather have one night of wonderful with him than a lifetime of average with someone else had taken a bit more doing. Yet that little voice in her head still held out hope that he might recognize her feelings and change.

She was doing the stupid-woman thing. Men pick women hoping they won't change and women pick men hoping they will. She was about to willingly and knowingly enter into a dead-end relationship that could only end one way—badly.

She placed her hands flat against his chest and gave a little shove. "Maybe we're moving a little too fast. Maybe this is wrong."

"How can you say that?" he countered.

She watched him from behind the safety of her lashes. "I don't do this sort of thing. I don't usually sleep around just for the hell of it."

"Val," he said her name in a rush of breath and confusion. "I don't want to make love to you for the hell of it. I will stop, if that's what you want."

"I thought I knew what I wanted," she said.

He looked at her with eyes so full of tenderness she almost wept.

He brushed his lips across her forehead. "I find you an incredible mixture of strength and vulnerability. I've never been this off balance with a woman and it has nothing to do with the recent events in my life."

"I guess we don't really need a reason. We *are* good friends. That has to matter."

"Tell yourself whatever you want, Val," he insisted as his fingers moved to grip her upper arms. His lips touched hers. He kissed her lightly. "Friends, huh? Well, I enjoy the way you laugh. I like the fire in your eyes when you're angry. I think I even like the way you've rejected me during the last six years."

"Chance?" she whispered, feeling her confidence crumble. After words like those, she knew she shouldn't take this next step. She started to push out of his embrace.

"Don't, Val, please. I know it will be incredible between us and I don't think I can go on pretending I'm happy with the occasional crumb you toss at me."

"They aren't crumbs," she insisted. "I know you don't want complications, but I—"

He silenced her by kissing her with equal

measures of passion and pleading. "Be quiet and trust me."

"This wasn't what I planned," she admitted. "You're confusing me."

"I'm trying not to," he said quietly. His hand came up and he captured a lock of her hair between his thumb and forefinger. He silently studied the dark strands, his expression intense.

"I don't know what to do, Chance. I don't want to make a mistake. I don't want to be hurt."

"We're a little beyond that, so let's just see where this leads. Overanalyzing things never yields the results you need and usually keeps you from having the things you want," he cautioned, his voice low and seductive.

The honesty and sincerity in his voice worked like a vise on her throat. The lump of emotion threatened to strangle her as the moments of silence dragged on.

"We don't have anything in common. We want different things."

"We'll talk about it later," he said as he scooped her off the floor, cradling her against his solid chest.

Chance carried her upstairs to her bedroom. As if she were some fragile object, he placed her on the bed, gently arranging her against the pillows.

Val remained silent as she watched him shrug out of his shirt before joining her on the bed. Through passion-dilated eyes, she took in the impressive sight of him. Rolling on his side, Chance pulled her closer, until she encountered the solid outline of his body. His expression was fixed, his mouth little more than a taut line.

"I'll erase those worry lines, Val. You'll see," he said as he gently pulled her into the circle of his arms.

It felt so good, so right. She needed this, needed his strength if she was going to make it through this without losing her mind. Closing her eyes, Val reminded herself that she would know what it was like to connect with him—at least for one night.

She surrendered to the promise she felt in his touch.

Cradling her in one arm, Chance used his free hand to stroke the hair away from her face. She greedily drank in the scent of his cologne as she cautiously allowed her fingers to rest against his thigh. His skin was warm and smooth, a startling contrast to the very defined muscle she could feel beneath her hand. She remained perfectly still, comforted by his scent, his touch and his nearness. Being here with Chance was enough to erase the fear and uncertainty that had plagued her. What could be the harm in just a few hours of the pleasure she knew she could find here?

"Val?" he asked on a strained breath. He captured her face in his hands. His thumbs teased her cheekbones. His darkened eyes met and held hers. His jaw set, his expression serious. "I don't know if I have the strength to get up and walk away from you now. Please tell me this is what you want. Please?"

Using his hands, he tilted her head back. His face was mere fractions of an inch from hers. She could feel the ragged expulsion of his breath. Instinctively, her palms flattened against his chest. The thick mat of dark hair served as a cushion for her touch. Still, beneath the softness, she could easily feel the hard outline of muscle.

"I want you so badly," he said in a near whisper.

Her lashes fluttered as his words washed over her upturned face. She needed to hear those words, perhaps had even wished for them in that secret part of her heart. Chance's lips tentatively brushed hers. So featherlight was the kiss that she wasn't even certain it could qualify as such. His movements were careful, measured. His thumbs stroked the hollows of her cheeks.

Val banished all thought from her mind. She wanted this, desperately. The feel of his hands and his lips made her feel alive. The ache in her chest was changing, evolving. The fear and confusion were being taken over by some new emotions.

She became acutely aware of every aspect of him. The pressure of his thigh where it touched hers. The sound of his uneven breathing. The magical sensation of his mouth on hers.

When he lifted his head, Val grabbed his broad shoulders. "Don't," she whispered, urging him back to her. "I do want this, Chance. I want you."

His resistance was both surprising and short-lived. It was almost totally forgotten when he dipped his head. His lips did more than brush against hers. His hands left her face and wound around her small body. Chance crushed her against him. She could actually feel the pounding of his heart beneath her hands.

The encounter quickly turned into something intense and consuming. His tongue moistened her slightly parted lips. The kiss became demanding and she was a very willing participant. She managed to work her hands across his chest, until she felt the outline of his erect nipples beneath her palms. He responded to her action by running his hands all over her back and nibbling her lower lip. It was a purely erotic action, one that inspired great need and desire in her.

A small moan escaped her lips as she kneaded the muscles of his chest. He tasted vaguely of mint and he continued to work magic with his mouth. Val felt the kiss in the pit of her stomach. What had started as a pleasant warmth had grown into a full-fledged heat emanating from her very core, fueled by the sensation of his fingers snaking up her back, entwining in her hair and guiding her head back at a severe angle. Passion flared as he hungrily devoured first her mouth, then the tender flesh at the base of her throat. His mouth was hot, the stubble of his beard slightly abrasive. And she felt it all. She was aware of everything—the outline of his body, the almost arrogant expectation in his kiss. Chance was a skilled and amazing lover—Val, a compliant and demanding partner.

This was a wondrous new place for her, special and beautiful. The controlled urgency of his need was a heady thing. It gave Val the sense that she had a certain primal power over this beautiful man.

Chance made quick work of her clothes. He kissed, touched and tasted until Val literally cried out for their joining. It was no longer an act; it was a need. She needed Chance inside her to feel complete. To feel connected.

Poised above her, his brow glistening with perspiration, Chance looked down at her with smoldering, heavy eyes. He waited for her to guide him, and then filled her with one long, powerful thrust.

The sights and sounds around her became a blur as the knot in her stomach wound tighter with each passing minute. Building fiercely until she felt the spasm of satisfaction begin to wrack her body. Chance groaned against her ear as he joined her in release.

As her heart rate returned to normal, her mind was anything but. She lay there perfectly still, not sure what to do or say. She'd made love to Chance with total and complete abandon. The experience was wild, primitive. Her eyes fluttered in the darkness as she began to think of the consequences of her rash behavior.

Guilt swept over her like a blanket as she realized the gravity of the situation. All she could do now was wait for him to fall asleep so she could be alone with her own recriminations. She'd started a reluctant roll out of the sanctuary of his arms when the phone rang.

Chapter Seventeen

"My license is in my wallet, in my purse, which I don't have," Val screamed.

"I'll take you," Chance offered, shrugging into his clothes. "A doctor might come in handy since you're going to deliver Leta's baby."

"I don't need sarcasm," Val retorted hotly. *I need mood-altering drugs or a magic potion to erase the last hour from my memory. Good lord! What was I thinking?*

"Don't bite my head off because you're second-guessing yourself."

"I can do anything I want," Val promised him. "Isn't that the true definition of a non-involved involvement?"

"You could have said no any time along the way."

Cringing inwardly, Val summoned her intellect and pushed everything else to the back burner. "You're right, Chance. Sorry."

"We can talk about it if you want."

"No thanks." Hopping, she managed to get her foot into her shoe. "Ready?"

"One second."

Seeing him in her bedroom, hair mussed, shirt open, zipping his fly made her move faster than normal. She raced downstairs and waited for him to join her outside.

The drive to the reservation included uncomfortable fits and starts of conversation. The subject was irrelevant.

His headlights were the only source of light around. "Do you have your phone?" Val asked.

"In the glove compartment," Chance said.

Retrieving the phone, Val called to check on Leta. The poor girl's voice was strained and she was whimpering, but Val was pretty sure part of that was fear.

"How far apart are your contractions?" she asked.

"Fifteen minutes. About."

"Breathe, Leta. We should be there in about thirty minutes."

"Thirty minutes?"

"You've got time," Val reassured her. "Think happy thoughts and give the phone to your mom." Val recited Chance's cell number and promised to call back when they were closer to the reservation.

"I guess suggesting she go to the hospital is out of the question?" Chance asked.

"Aside from the fact that she has no insurance, Leta is determined to have a home birth. A decision she might regret if she knew how wonderful an epidural could be."

"Was that the Queen of Natural Medicine promoting a chemical fix?"

"You betcha." Val laughed. "I've attended enough births to conclude that the drugs should be potent and free-flowing."

"And miss the wonder of childbirth?"

"Not the wonder, the incredible pain." She shivered at the mere thought.

"Are you the same woman who wanted to walk away from a hit-and-run?"

"I was unconscious for a lot of that," she reminded him.

"I'm sure you'll do fine when it's your turn."

"Something like that," she muttered. This thing with Chance wouldn't lead down that road. There was no wedding in her future. No children. Hell, there was no future.

Chance cursed, and then she heard the tires squeal and felt the car swerve as he stomped on the brakes.

Looking ahead, she surveyed the road ahead. What was left of a motorcycle lay bent and twisted near the shoulder. A little further down the incline, she spotted the curled figure of its rider.

"There's a flashlight in the glove compartment. Call for an ambulance. I'll get my bag."

Working in perfect harmony, Val anticipated Chance's moves and helped him turn the injured man on to his back. He let out a yelp of pain and grabbed his thigh.

"Open fracture," Chance said.

Thankfully, his helmet had protected his head, but the accident had snapped his calf like a twig. Val gave him a comforting smile and wiped some dirt away from his mouth.

"I can't see enough. Can you move the car?"

Scrambling to her feet, Val steered the SUV into place, maneuvering the front end so that the high beams shone directly on the injured man. She was just setting the emergency brake when she saw Chance reach into his bag.

Leaping from the car, she was about to call to him when apparently Chance had reached the same conclusion.

He stood and walked over to the car. "The guy is in agony, but I'm afraid to give him morphine."

Val nodded.

Chance punched the side of his car. "Ouch!"

"Now you're both in pain. What did that prove?" she asked dryly.

They huddled together, making sure their voices were low. Chance felt completely helpless and he didn't like that feeling one bit. He was pretty damned useless on all fronts. He had the knowledge and training to help the poor guy with the bone sticking out of his skin, but he didn't dare use the vial in his bag without knowing what it contained. It could be fine or it could be acid. He wasn't about to risk the guy's life when an ambulance was on its way.

He had been nothing but straightforward with Val. *So how come I feel like I'm a bastard?* he wondered.

Chance went back to his patient to explain

what was going to happen. "You've got to keep still."

"Hurts like hell," the man responded through clenched teeth.

"They'll have something on the ambulance to take the edge off."

"I thought you were a doctor," the guy argued. "Can't you do something?"

"I don't want to do more harm than good," he admitted. Thankfully, he heard the wail of a siren cut through the night. At about the same time, the cell phone rang.

He watched as Val placed one hand over her ear in order to hear above the approaching noise.

"Leta's seven minutes apart."

"Go!" Chance insisted, tossing her the keys.

"It's not legal. I don't have a license."

"I don't think Leta will care. Don't worry about it, just go."

Chance worked with the paramedics while Val went off to the reservation. He was sorry he hadn't wished her well.

"Coming with us?" one paramedic asked.

Chance nodded and hopped into the back of the ambulance. They covered the thirty miles in less than twenty minutes. By the time they arrived at the ambulance bay, the man was blissfully under the influence of an intravenous painkiller.

Seth was waiting for him in the hallway of the emergency room. "Out drumming up business?"

"Found him on the side of the road."

"Where's Val?"

"Delivering a baby."

Seth whistled. "I can see you took my advice about laying low to heart."

Chance handed the medical bag to his brother. "I keep this in my car for emergencies."

"I know."

"I want the stuff in there tested, just to be safe."

"Good idea," Seth agreed. "Let's have it done here. No sense in waiting for the state lab."

"Thanks."

"Did you have an accident, too?"

"No," Chance answered, falling in step with his brother. "Why?"

"Your shirt is buttoned wrong."

Glancing down, Chance cursed under his breath. "I got dressed in the dark."

"Do I want to hear this?" Seth asked.

Chance was careful to keep his voice to a near whisper. "Probably not, but I need you to answer me one question."

"Shoot."

"If Val came on to you, would you have slept with her?"

"I'm happily married."

"Not now." Chance felt like smacking Seth. "I mean before."

"Val would never have come on to me."

"Seth! Stop being an annoyance and give me some brotherly advice."

Seth stopped and turned, squaring off. "Forgetting for a minute that I really don't want to be having this conversation."

"Yeah, yeah."

"I'm sorry, Chance. I think you screwed up. You know what kind of woman Val is and you know she has feelings for you."

"I don't know that."

Seth glared at him. "You do know it, Chance. Not admitting it isn't the same as not knowing it. You knew it and you acted anyway."

"It was her idea!"

"And you were helplessly tied to the bed-post?" Seth returned hotly. "You know the drill, Chance. You never, ever have sex with a woman who loves you if you can't return the feelings."

"Who says I can't."

Seth looked as shocked as Chance felt. "Do you love her?"

"Yeah. Probably."

"Then you screwed up even worse."

"How?"

"Never, ever sleep with a woman you love if you don't plan to stick it out."

"Who says I don't?"

Seth grunted, clearly frustrated. "Fine. Last rule—never, ever tell your older brother that you love a woman before you've told her yourself."

"You're no help."

"You've got to figure this one out on your own." Seth's pager bleeped to life. He read the display, then said, "Let's drop this off and go to my office. The fingerprint unit has found something."

LETA'S HOUSE was a bustling hub of activity. Every relative, regardless of how remote the bloodline, must have been camped in or around the small home.

Val was greeted like some sort of head of state as she hurried toward the front door.

Leta was in the back bedroom, surrounded by her mother and five other women. Her young husband was seated in the corner, looking completely overwhelmed by the whole situation.

"How is it going?"

Leta's dark hair was matted with perspiration. Her dark eyes were wide, as was her smile. "I'm glad you're here."

"Sorry about the delay." Val opened the small bag she had left with Leta and took out the gloves, clamps and other items she might need. "Ready to have a baby?"

Leta nodded. "For about the last seven hours."

"Great things are worth waiting for."

"Like your doctor?" Leta's mother asked.

Val just shrugged. Chance was not and would never be hers. "We've got work to do."

Leta's husband regrouped and by the time

she was completing her second hour of pushing, he was her best cheerleader.

"Okay, Leta," Val began, "you'll be a mom with the next push."

"Promise?"

"Absolutely. Listen to me, though. Ready?"

Leta didn't just push, she screamed her baby into the world. It was a moment of pure joy. The tiny little boy was perfect in every way.

"You did it!" Blinking back her own tears, Val laughed and placed the wet, wiggling little guy on his mother's belly. "You sure did."

She was only vaguely aware of the group cheer that went up outside her. Val listened to the baby's heart and lungs, then spent some time making sure mother and son no longer needed air.

"Does he have a name?" she asked.

Leta was beaming. "Austin."

"That's nice."

"It was my maiden name and I want my son to have it."

Val smiled. "That's a nice tradition." The cell phone rang and Leta's mother passed it to her. "Hello?"

"So does the reservation have a new resident yet?"

The sound of Chance's voice felt perfect just then. "He arrived about a half hour ago. I'm guessing he's an eight-pounder."

"You did good, Val."

She looked over at the giddy new family. "Yes, I did."

"I'm at Seth's office. We're waiting for a report about the space heater."

"I'll come back in a bit."

"Stay there," Chance insisted. "Get some sleep. It will be light in a few hours. You can drive back in the morning."

"What about you?"

"I've got an idea I'm going to have Seth check on."

Chapter Eighteen

"I told you not to drive back," Chance repeated when Val came through Seth's office door.

"Hello to you, too," she greeted. "I wouldn't have come back if you wouldn't have been so evasive."

"I wasn't evasive," Chance insisted. "I just knew Seth couldn't get the information immediately."

"What information?"

"The heater didn't have any fingerprints on it," he explained.

"Sorry," she offered.

"That isn't necessarily a bad thing. It pretty much proves that it was planted."

She smiled at him. "I never thought otherwise." She yawned. "So what is your idea?"

"Since someone had to go to a lot of trouble to get a car matching mine, I figure it's probably rented. Seth is checking with all the car places."

"Excellent," she said. "Anything else?"

Chance dipped his head so he spoke close to her ear. "We should talk."

"I'm on hour twenty of a twenty-four-hour day. Can't it wait?"

"No. Let's go to my place, it's closest."

They left Seth to wait for the reports on rental cars. Chance's nerves were strained. It wasn't fatigue; it was an emotional kind of energy overloading his seriously stressed system.

"Am I going to need coffee for this?" Val asked, throwing herself on his settee and curling into a fetal position. "I've brought new life into the world. Even God got a break after he did that."

"Sit up. I'll try to be quick."

He tugged her into a sitting position, then quickly joined her to prevent her from lying down again.

"I've been thinking," he began.

"We're really going to have this conversation now?" she asked him wearily. "We can skip it and I can just send myself the flowers tomorrow."

He touched her cheek and looked into her eyes. "You think that's what I wanted to say?"

"This is me, Chance. Remember? I know you and I knew what I was doing."

He found her easy willingness to expect so little of him annoying. "I'm enlightened now and I'm trying to share some of my enlightenment. So you wanna cut me some slack?"

She shifted away from him. "Can't we just pretend it didn't happen?"

"No. I told Seth."

Her drowsy eyes opened wide. "Why?"

"I needed to talk to someone."

"Don't you know you're not supposed to kiss and tell?"

Chance felt himself frown. "How did this turn into a discussion about Seth? I wasn't discussing details. I just had some things to work out, so I spoke—discreetly, I might add—to my brother."

"I wish you wouldn't have done that."

He was surprised. "Why?"

"Because I would have preferred to keep my sex life private. And because I'm sure I know Seth's reaction."

"Really?"

She nodded. "He probably suggested something completely wrong, like you should try to pledge your undying love to me."

His annoyance grew. "You said that as if it left a bad taste in your mouth."

"It does," she insisted. "Don't you get it?"

"Apparently not," he admitted.

"A relationship with you isn't what I want."

"But you've always said—"

She raised her hand to silence him. "I've always said I wanted the fairy tale and I do. You going to Seth just proves that you aren't ready."

"I wasn't going to propose tonight," Chance shot back.

"And I never asked you to," she replied with equal force. "What makes you think I want to settle?"

"I think you're in love with me."

To her credit, Val didn't gasp in horror, though she did cringe and he noted a healthy dose of pride in her eyes as her back stiffened regally.

"I don't have any control over that, Chance. But I can get over it. At least I'm willing to be honest about my feelings."

"What do you call what I'm doing?"

"Guilt," she answered frankly.

"Of course I'm feeling guilty. Aren't you even a little sorry that we're destroying a great friendship?"

She stood and peered down at him. "Yes, Chance. I truly wish it had never happened. It did. But this won't. How I feel about you isn't relevant."

"Why not?"

"Because I'm a big girl and I'll get over this. What's the alternative? Us getting together and me wondering every second of every day if you were with me only because your big brother guilted you into it? Pass, thanks. I have way too much self-respect for that." She took a couple of breaths, then continued. "I appreciate that you're trying to do the right thing here. But this isn't it. The best thing you can do for me now is just give it some space."

VAL TRIED not to think about the wounded look on Chance's face when he had dropped her at home. Trying wasn't succeeding.

After managing a few hours of fitful sleep, she was doing nothing but pacing around her house. She checked and rechecked all the doors and windows. Her dilemma with Chance was painful, but dead was forever and the crazy person was still on the loose.

When the phone rang, she hoped it was Chance and prayed it wasn't. "Hello?"

"It's Seth. How's everything?"

"Fine," she lied, blushing as she remembered that he knew the most intimate detail of her life.

"Do you know anyone named Hartley?"

"Yeah," she answered. "Hang on while I boot my computer." It took her less than a minute to open the correct file. "I've got a Teresa Hartley—she was a patient of Chance's."

"We've got something. Know where I can find her?"

"Why are you asking about Mrs. Hartley?" She could tell Seth wasn't alone and was pretty certain Chance was the muffled voice she heard peppering questions in the background.

"She rented a black SUV matching Chance's the same afternoon as the heater incident."

"Not likely," Val replied. "She died almost two years ago. I remember her. Nice lady. There were complications from her diabetes."

Chance's voice suddenly came on the line. "I was right?" he asked.

"You remember her. She wouldn't follow her diet, missed appointments and failed to check her insulin?"

"Did she have a husband?" Chance asked.

"Widowed," Val answered. "I've got to go to the office to get the complete file. Do you want me to do that?"

"If you don't mind. I've got to go to hospital to light a fire under them. They still haven't tested the drugs in my bag and Seth wants everything sent for prints."

"I'm happy to help."

"Val, I—"

She heard the catch in his voice and responded by saying, "We really can still be friends."

"I need that," he said, then broke the connection.

She figured even if she got a ticket for driving without a license, she could have Seth testify on her behalf. After all, she was working for Chance.

It took her no time to get down to the office at midday. Hurriedly, she slipped her key into the lock and pushed inside, flipping light switches as she went.

She turned on the computer and, not trusting its reliability in light of recent events, she went into the storage area to dig out the hard copies, as well.

There wasn't anything notable in the computer system, so she blew dust off the cover of the folder and started to read from the beginning.

Save for the diabetes, Mrs. Hartley wasn't a frequent patient. Her file dated back to a couple of years before Chance took over the practice. Val recognized the former doctor's handwriting and easily found the point in time when Chance began managing her disease.

Hearing a car out front, she looked up expecting Chance. Instead, she spotted Tara walking toward the door, cradling something in her arms. Val started to stand and in doing so, dropped an envelope from between the pages of the medical chart.

She picked it up off the floor at the same time Tara entered the office.

"Hi," she called, glancing down at the typed address on the envelope.

"You here alone? I didn't see Dr. Landry's car."

"He won't be here for a while," Val returned, her attention drawn to the cat in Tara's arms. "You found him!" she cried. "I don't know why I care so much, the thing isn't very loyal."

"He's male, what do you expect?"

"So true," Val agreed, reaching for the animal. "I missed you, too," she told him as he jumped from her arms and disappeared into the back hallway. Returning to her seat, she offered Tara a broad smile. "I'm really sorry about running in front of you the other day."

"Don't mention it," Tara said. "You really shouldn't be here without locking the doors."

It was a public building on a public street, and Val doubted she was in imminent danger. Still, Tara was right to be cautious, so she didn't complain when she bolted the door.

"I think there's a stack of payments on Chance's desk," she said as she returned to her chore. Sticking her finger beneath the flap of the envelope, she retrieved the note card and began to read. It was dated a year before Mrs. Hartley died.

Dear Dr. Landry:
This is in reference to my mother-in-law, Teresa Hartley. I am no longer married to her daughter and therefore, no longer interested in or obligated, morally or otherwise, to pay her medical bills.

"Nice guy," she muttered, then continued to read.

Any further communications should be sent to my ex-wife, at the address below. Respectfully,

"Ira M. Bishop." Val looked up in time to see Tara with a gun trained in her direction.

"I'M SURE, Dr. Landry."
Chance looked down at the printout again.

"I would have killed that guy in a matter of minutes."

"The percentage makes that big a difference?" Seth asked.

"The difference between 0.5 grams of morphine and 50 grams of morphine is kind of like the difference between a water gun and an infrared ballistic missile."

"That I understand," Seth said.

"Can you do a background check on Teresa Hartley?" Chance asked.

Seth answered in the affirmative, so they went back to his office. Chance sat at his brother's desk while Seth worked with one of the deputies on getting the information.

He tried the office, but got the service instead. They said Val hadn't been answering the phone all morning. She was probably waist-deep in the old files. Knowing her as he did, he was sure she could find anything that was even remotely relevant.

Bored, he began to glance at the photographs from the hit-and-run. One was a close-up of the pavement with a few drops of blood.

His heart seized when he saw it. The image of Val on that ground still haunted him. He looked at the ceiling and wondered if some divine wisdom might drop into his lap. Apparently not. There was no simple solution to the current mess that was his life.

It was dangerous, complicated and...

Simple.

He loved Val. It wasn't based on guilt or anything else. He couldn't imagine his life without her in it. Especially seeing such a vivid reminder of how close to reality that had been. He glanced again at the pictures, then focused on one in particular.

Staring at the image, he felt the blood run cold in his veins. "Seth!"

"I've got something," his brother said as he came in.

"The skid marks didn't start until a foot or more after where the truck was parked," Chance said on a rush. "Val didn't run into Tara Bishop."

"Well, that doesn't surprise me after what I just found out. According to vital records, Teresa Hartley had one child, a daughter, named Tara."

"I just called the office. Val didn't answer."

"Try the cell," Seth insisted.

Chance was so consumed with fear and dread that he had a difficult time remembering the number.

It wasn't until he heard the voice on the other end that he realized he had been holding his breath. "Val?"

"She's tied up right now."

"Tara, listen," he began.

"No, no! You listen."

He angled the small phone so that Seth could hear, as well.

"I'm listening."

"I'll call you back in an hour."

"Why an hour?"

"That should be enough time for the drugs to take effect. I'll call you back so you can listen to her die."

Chapter Nineteen

"You aren't thinking straight," Val argued, twisting her hands so that she might be able to reach the nylon bindings.

Tara was behind the wheel. She appeared calm and eerily serene. "I've thought this through completely," Tara assured her. "I've been more than patient, don't you agree?"

"I can't agree because I don't know what *this* is. I was talking about me. I'm hardly appropriate bait for Chance."

"You're perfect," Tara argued. "Especially once you interfered with what I had planned originally." She turned on to a dirt road.

Val was being jostled around on the uneven surface and was unable to steady herself with her hands tied behind her back.

"And you aren't bait. I have no intention of luring Chance anywhere."

"Then why are you doing this?"

"I want him to suffer."

"Why?"

"So he'll know what it feels like. My mother suffered from his neglect and died. I have to live with that. Now Chance will have to live with knowing Dora's death was his fault and Moe Mackey's and Kent Dawson, too, if Benton hadn't picked up the error so quickly."

"Your mother suffered from a disease that is sometimes fatal."

"Diabetes is treatable," Tara insisted as she slowed the car and parked behind a weathered shack in the middle of nowhere.

Scanning the area, Val knew where they were. They were near the abandoned Weller Emerald Mine. The dirt road leading in stopped just beyond the shack. That kind of dashed any hope she had of someone stumbling upon her. She had to think. In thirty minutes, Chance was going to call back and she was pretty certain Tara meant to make good on her promise.

"I SHOULD WAIT for a warrant," Seth said just before the two of them kicked down the door to Tara's apartment.

"Not here!" Seth called.

"That would have been too easy."

The small apartment was neat and orderly, except for a wall montage of photographs that hinted at the true depths of Tara's venom.

There were pictures of Chance dating back more than a year. Taken everywhere from in front of his office to one from the road above the beach house in Mexico where he vacationed in February.

"This is pretty damned sick," Seth opined.

"There's got to be something here to tell us where she's taken Val."

With his brother's help, Chance began ripping apart the top dresser drawer. He had gone through three others before finding anything. "Sick and smart. A dangerous combination." He handed Seth a copy of the Mensa Society membership card he'd found beneath some clothing. "How much time?"

"A half hour," Seth answered. "Look at this."

Chance went over to the desk and took the map. "There must be fifty places circled here."

The crude little smiley face drawn in the center made his blood boil. Tara obviously realized they would be on to her and she made sure not to leave anything incriminating behind. At least nothing obvious.

"She used her mother's identity to rent the car, right?" Chance asked.

"I'll alert the transit department."

Chance saw a bulge of brown leather sticking out from under the bed. "That's Val's purse."

Yanking it free, he dumped the contents on the bed. "There's no wallet."

"She can't pass herself off as Val. The descriptions don't match."

"If she can fake hospital orders complete with signatures, I'm sure she can dummy up identification."

Seth revised the alert to include any reservations or purchases in Val's name.

Chance continued to tear at the apartment while fear over what Val might be enduring tore at his insides.

"Fifteen minutes until you have to make

the call," Seth quietly warned. "The choppers are up and all we can do is hope she trips up and gives us an idea of where she is."

"This woman won't make a stupid mistake like that," Chance countered, rubbing his hands in his hair as he willed his brain to conjure something. There was no way in hell he would sit back and do nothing while Val's life was at stake.

"She likes to play games," Chance said aloud. He grabbed the map. "I'm sure one of these circles is where she has Val. Tara wants me to suffer knowing I had the location in my hand the whole time."

"Speaking of which," Seth reminded solemnly, "I can send out every available unit and the choppers but that's a lot of ground to cover."

"I'll get her talking," Chance said. "I'll try to buy time for us. I can't let anything happen to Val."

SHE WAS SEATED in a single chair in the center of the room. The air was musty and thick with dust, but that probably wouldn't be a problem for long. Tara wasn't far away, fill-ing a syringe. The gun was by her left foot but Val knew there wasn't any way for her to reach the weapon first.

"Benzodiazepine," Tara announced. "Wonderful little compound. It can ease the ill effects of cancer treatments and is often given as a pre-surgical drug to keep patients calm."

"I know what it does," Val breathed. She was trying to keep her fear in check as she watched Tara flick the syringe and squirt a small amount of the drug from the tip.

"I'm very good at injections. I used to have to help my mother."

"Let's get back to that," Val suggested.

The phone rang. Tara answered it. "You're early."

Step away from the gun.

"But I'm flexible. I'll just move up my timetable."

Tara was frowning, apparently not pleased with whatever Chance said. She partially covered the mouthpiece and turned to Val. "He's threatening me. Under the circumstances, I would think he would be a little more...respectful." She returned her attention to the phone. "Five more minutes, Chance." She flipped the phone closed.

Val heard a helicopter in the distance, but then, so did Tara. She didn't seem fazed.

"That's my cue to move things along," Tara sighed. "Good night, Val."

"Sheriff Landry?"

"Go ahead," he called into the open radio.

"We got a hit on a rental at AirWorld for a Valerie Greene out of Killington Field."

Chance felt his head about to explode. That was nearly fifty miles away. "When is she set to take off?"

"It's in the air now," the dispatcher said. "I can patch you through to the pilot."

"Do it!"

Glancing at his watch, Chance knew time was running out.

"Seventeen-Fox-Charlie. Over."

Seth identified himself, then asked. "What is your location and flight plan? Over!"

"A mile out from Weller Mine. Private party charter to West Helena Air Terminal. Over."

Seth's foot smashed the accelerator. "Do not pick up the charter. Copy. Over."

"Wait!" Chance's mind raced. "If Tara's got Val out at Weller's, she's already heard the chopper. She could freak and kill Val if anything happens."

"Copy abort charter. Returning to terminal. Over."

"No!" Chance screamed into the radio. "Zigzag, do something, but don't turn away. Just hang on, okay?"

"Roger that."

"How long until we get there?" Chance asked.

"Two minutes."

"I've got about thirty seconds. Any suggestions?"

"Pray."

Chance held the phone cupped against his mouth. He didn't dare risk Tara hearing anything that might alert her to the fact that they knew where she was. He dialed the number just as Seth brought the car to a halt a few yards shy of the building.

"Hello, Chance. Very punctual."

"I try," he answered. "This is your show and all, but can you explain a couple of things to me?"

"Sorry, not in the plan."

Silently, he mouthed instructions to Seth. He needed the helicopter to land while he was creeping through the high grasses.

"What is the plan?"

"There's probably enough time for you to say goodbye before poor Val nods off to sleep."

"Chance?"

He barely recognized Val's weak voice. "Hang on, sweetheart."

"I'm going to see *The Wizard of Oz,*" she slurred into the phone.

Chance was impressed. Mainly because he had reached the side of the shack and could now see inside. Tara had the phone to Val's ear and she appeared to be slouched and struggling to remain in the seat. There was a discarded syringe on the floor.

"What'd she give you, Val?"

"Benzo—"

Tara snatched the phone and he had to jerk back for fear she might see him. The nearby helicopter was deafening, as was the sight of the gun at Tara's side.

"No fair, Val. I didn't want her to tell you

what I'd given her." Tara was screaming to be heard above the noise.

"Val's always had a mind of her own."

"Oh well, on the off chance that you managed to get lucky and reach Val before the drug could take effect, I had a backup. Not as neat or as creative. But then, neither was the car accident. That was an opportunity seized, don't you agree?"

"Actually, I thought it was pretty amateurish."

"You wound me, Chance. But, I guess that's fair since I'm about to put a big wound in Val's skull."

The helicopter that had provided cover was now interference. If he opened the door, Tara would be alerted by the noise and there was no way to reach her before she pulled the trigger. He motioned to Seth. "You're going to kill another innocent person because your mother didn't take her medicine?"

"That was your job," she growled. "You stopped treating her because my creep of an ex-husband stopped paying you. Does that fifty-dollar office-visit fee you couldn't collect seem important now?"

"You've got it all wrong, Tara. Your mother didn't keep her appointments. And you're about to kill the woman who used to go and see your mother, begging her to watch her diet and monitor her blood sugar. By the way, why weren't you taking care of your mother? Where were you?"

"I was entitled to a life!" Tara shot back. "I spent the first eighteen years of my life taking care of her. I married a jerk just to get a break from the responsibility."

Chance noticed that Val had completely stopped moving. Seth had come up beside him, weapon drawn. Tara raised her hands and took aim.

"I circled the place where you can find Val's remains. Good luck."

The last syllable still hung in the thick air above her head when Val called on the last of her strength. She tucked and lunged to the side, just as the acrid smell of gun smoke filled her nostrils.

"Val!"

She wanted to open her eyes, but they simply wouldn't cooperate. "Am I d-dead?"

"Dumb, not dead," Chance answered suddenly by her side. She had no idea how he had found her—and she didn't care.

"What were you thinking? She had a gun."

"Not ready to die," she answered. Each word seemed stuck on her tongue. Val tried to smile but she could no longer feel the muscles in her face. "You found me."

"Yes, I did. Dammit! Seth! I'm losing her pulse! Go commandeer that helicopter!"

Epilogue

"You did a really good thing," she told Dr. Benton when she opened her eyes and saw him at the foot of her bed.

His smile was apologetic. "It wasn't me, Val. Chance breathed for you when you went into respiratory failure."

"I know. I was talking about Kent Dawson," she clarified, then repeated what she had learned from Tara. "If you hadn't diagnosed the iodine allergy so quickly, he would have died."

Benton shrugged. "I like to think I'm a good doctor."

"You are," she said on a smile. "And a lucky one, too."

"Why is that?"

"You have a great life. Your wife adores

you. You have two beautiful kids, an established career that you love. You've got it all."

Benton blushed. "I guess I do."

"Are you bothering my patient, Dr. Benton?" Chance asked as he peeked through the door.

"Nope. She was just reminding me of some very important facts."

"She's annoying that way."

Chance held the door for Benton before entering the room. He cradled a box under his arm. In a very uncharacteristic move, he walked over and kissed her on the mouth.

"I'm not annoying," she said against his lips.

"Are, too."

"You called me dumb at the mine shack and now annoying. You should be nicer to the woman you almost got killed."

He winced. "That's going to hang there like an albatross between us, isn't it?"

"It's a pretty big thing, Chance. But thanks to my sharp mind and quick wit, Tara won't be able to hurt anyone else."

"Aren't you forgetting something that is very important in all this?"

"My present?" she suggested, making a failed attempt to grab it out of his hand.

Chance sat on the edge of her bed. His smile was warm and comforting.

"No. The way I risked life and limb to bravely tackle and disarm her so that I could rescue you in the nick of time."

Val chuckled. "Thank you, brave sir, but the truth of the matter is, I just didn't want to get shot."

His smile broadened and his dark eyes flashed. "You're putting a cramp in my fairy-tale-ending scenario."

Val swallowed nervously. "We both know you aren't the fairy-tale type."

"I've changed," he said, presenting her with the elaborately wrapped gift. "This is for the brave princess."

With no pretense of patience, Val ripped into the pink paper and tore off the top.

"I thought princesses were supposed to be reserved and well-mannered."

"You thought wrong," Val teased. "A tiara," she commented, pulling the rhinestone-en-crusted thing out of the box. "Most people would have brought flowers or candy."

His expression stilled. "I'm not most people, Val."

She opened her mouth, but he placed his fingertip to her lips. "This isn't guilt or gratitude or anything. The truth is, I love you. I think I've known that deep down since I came running out of the café and found you on the ground."

"But you don't want—"

"I'm telling you what I want," he insisted as he reached into his pocket and produced a small, velvet box. "I want to share my life with you. I want to have children with you and grow old with you. I want to fight and make up and—"

"You have to be sure."

He rolled his eyes and smiled as he opened the box. "I am sure, Val. We've been through more together in the last few days than most people experience in a lifetime. I don't want to end up like Tara. Before you, I was probably headed in that direction."

"You're thinking of becoming a psychopathic killer?"

"No. I'm thinking more about the way her own regrets destroyed her because she didn't want to take responsibility for her own bad choices. I know absolutely that if I let you get away, I'll spend the rest of my life regretting it. Your love is a gift and I want to treasure it."

"There's only one problem."

"What?"

"I've never actually told you that I love you."

"Right," he agreed with a nod. "Well?"

"I'm thinking," she teased.

"Think too long and I'll take this ring back and exchange it for a smaller one."

"I love you."

He smiled down at her. "I think I could get to like this fairy-tale stuff."

"Well, then, this is the part of the story where you kiss me until my toes curl."

He did. And they did.